Just in time for June...
Janet Dailey's <u>The Hostage Bride</u>

It's been said that Janet Dailey "wrote the book" on romance. And Silhouette Books is thrilled to announce that Janet Dailey, America's best-loved romance author, will now be writing for Silhouette Romances, starting with *The Hostage Bride* in June.

You may have enjoyed one of Janet's recent novels: *Touch the Wind, The Rogue* or *Ride the Thunder.* All three made *The New York Times* best-seller list—and together sold well over three million copies! Her latest book, *Night Way*, is currently on the best-seller list, and is another million-seller.

More than eighty million people have already fallen in love with Janet Dailey. Her books have been translated into seventeen languages and are now sold in *ninety* different countries around the world.

We're sure that you too, will fall in love with Janet Dailey's romance novels. Be sure to watch for *The Hostage Bride* this June.

Dear Reader:

Silhouette Romances is an exciting new publishing venture. We will be presenting the very finest writers of contemporary romantic fiction as well as outstanding new talent in this field. It is our hope that our stories, our heroes and our heroines will give you, the reader, all you want from romantic fiction.

Also, *you* play an important part in our future plans for Silhouette Romances. We welcome any suggestions or comments on our books and I invite you to write to us at the address below.

So, enjoy this book and all the wonderful romances from Silhouette. They're for *you!*

Karen Solem
Editor-in-Chief
Silhouette Books
P. O. Box 769
New York, N.Y. 10019

JEANNE STEPHENS
Wonder and Wild Desire

Silhouette *Romance*

Published by Silhouette Books New York

America's Publisher of Contemporary Romance

Other Silhouette Romances by Jeanne Stephens

Mexican Nights

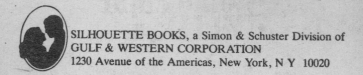

SILHOUETTE BOOKS, a Simon & Schuster Division of
GULF & WESTERN CORPORATION
1230 Avenue of the Americas, New York, N Y 10020

ISBN: 0-671-57080-3

First Silhouette printing May, 1981

10 9 8 7 6 5 4 3 2 1

America's Publisher of Contemporary Romance

Printed in the U S.A.

*For John K. Payne
with gratitude for his
continuing encouragement*

O lyric Love, half angel and half bird
And all a wonder and a wild desire.

—Robert Browning,
The Ring and the Book, bk. i

Chapter One

The day began as all weekdays did for Caroline Franklin. She bathed and dressed her ten-month-old nephew, Mike, fed him his oatmeal and orange juice, and carried him across the hall to the apartment of Mrs. Mawbrey, the widow who cared for him while Carrie was at work. She then took a city bus through Boise, arriving at the Simpson Car Agency a few minutes before eight-thirty, in time to make coffee in the office percolator before the arrival of Gladys Kincaide, the office manager.

Mr. Simpson came in about nine and went directly through the showroom to his office, calling a clipped "Morning," toward the glassed-in cubbyhole where Carrie and Gladys worked.

Carrie wasn't sure at what precise moment she began to feel uneasy. Gladys was unusually uncommunicative and hardly looked up from her ledgers and calculator. Mr. Simpson, who was ordinarily all over the place, remained closeted in his office, buzzing only once for Gladys to bring him his coffee. None of the salesmen came by to chat and joke as was their custom.

By lunchtime Carrie's intuition told her something was very much awry. She experienced a sense of doom hovering just above her head, and her imagination began to fabricate various potential catastrophes that might fall upon her at any moment. Mike must be all right or Mrs. Mawbrey would have phoned, she assured herself as she got her coat from the corner rack and prepared to go out for a hamburger.

"Can I bring you anything, Gladys?" she asked her co-worker, who was still bent over the ledgers.

"What? Oh, no, thanks, Carrie. I brought a sand-wich."

She put on her coat and left the cubbyhole-office to walk across the tiled showroom floor. Before she reached the entry, however, Mr. Simpson's office door opened and he thrust his balding head out.

"Carrie, I wonder if you would mind stepping into my office before you go to lunch. It will only take a moment."

"Certainly, Mr. Simpson." She joined him in the small paneled office.

"Please, sit down." He shut the door and walked around the desk to sit facing her.

She looked at him questioningly. Mr. Simpson—in his mid fifties and growing thick around the middle—had been extremely kind to her during the past thirteen months since she had come to work for the agency. There had been occasions when she had sensed that he was curious about her situation, the fact that she, twenty-one years old and unmarried, was raising her nephew alone. When she had brought Mike home from the hospital, she had taken a few days off to get things organized and find a baby-sitter. At that time she had told him merely that Mike's mother was dead and she had taken on the responsibility of caring for him. Beyond that, she had successfully avoided answering any questions from Mr. Simpson and the other people who worked at the agency.

Something in the way Mr. Simpson was looking at her now caused her uneasiness to increase. "Yes, sir?" she prompted as he settled back in his chair. He began shifting some papers about on his desk as if he had forgotten why he had asked her to come in—or, now that she was there, could not bring himself to broach the subject.

He laid the papers aside and leaned back, folding his hands across his thick waistline. "Carrie, this is one of the hardest things I've ever had to do, but—I'm going to have to let you go."

Carrie stared at him, certain momentarily that she had not understood correctly. Then she realized she *had* understood, and at last she knew the nature of the doom that she had sensed hovering about her all morning. Gladys and the salesmen had known, of course, and had been avoiding her. It was all so clear now.

The color drained from her face. "I—I don't understand, Mr. Simpson. You've never said that my work isn't satisfactory—"

"Oh, no, no," he interrupted her, his fleshy face going ruddy with distress and embarrassment. "It's nothing like that. You've done a good job here. Gladys has told me a number of times how bright you are, how much you have helped her in the office. But you are aware, I am sure, that car sales have been off for a couple of months now. All indications are that business will be slow right on through the winter."

"I see," she murmured, wishing that she could shut out his words, could somehow change the last few minutes. She ran slender fingers that had begun to shake through her dark brown hair and asked, "When do you want me to leave?"

The man winced visibly under the steady gaze of her blue-green eyes. "Today," he said finally. "Oh, I know I should have given you some warning, but I put off making this decision as long as I possibly could—hoping against hope that business would pick up. I know you have responsibilities. Gladys and I went over the books last week, looking for some way we could keep you." He sat forward, and there was earnest regret in his expression. "There isn't any. So—" He spread his blunt fingers, linking them together in front of him. "You might as well clean out your desk and leave now if you want. You have a week's vacation coming and two weeks' severance pay. Gladys will make out a check." He stared at his linked fingers for a moment, as if searching for another answer there, then met Carrie's vulnerable gaze. "I'm sorry, Carrie. Feel free to use my name as a reference on job applications. If you don't find something you want before spring, check back with me. I'll rehire you in a minute if business picks up."

"Thank you, Mr. Simpson," she said, coming out of the frightening jumble of her thoughts long enough to get to her feet and leave the office to return to the glassed-in cubicle. Gladys looked up from her ledgers as Carrie began taking her few personal belongings from her desk and stuffing them into her shoulder bag.

"He finally got up enough nerve to tell you, I guess," the middle-aged office manager said.

"Yes," Carrie replied, zipping her bag closed and turning to face Gladys. "He said you'd make out my check."

Gladys opened her desk drawer. "I already have. I'm sorry, Carrie. You're the best help I ever had in here. I don't know how I'll do it all without you."

Carrie tucked the check into the side pocket of her bag and managed a smile. "I've enjoyed working with you, Gladys. I'll miss you. Tell the salesmen goodbye for me."

She left the office and stepped out into the dreary November afternoon. Outside on a busy Boise street she clutched her bag and began to run in the direction of the bus stop, her open coat and dark brown hair flying out behind her. Halfway there, a sign penetrated her consciousness: *Café*. She halted and looked through the glass front. Seeing only a few customers, she walked in and took the most isolated table in the darkest corner, wanting to be alone for a few minutes so that she could recover her composure.

She ordered a grilled cheese sandwich and coffee, but when the order arrived she discovered that she was not hungry. The sandwich grew cold as she sat clenching the thick, warm mug in both hands. The feeling of desperate panic that had vibrated through her when Mr. Simpson told her she no longer had a job continued to plague her.

"Check back in the spring," he had said. For one crazy instant she had had to fight back hysterical laughter. Spring! She had barely managed to make ends meet the past ten months. Now she had three weeks' pay in her purse and no savings, and it was the worst possible time of the year to be looking for a secretarial job. There was a ten-month-old baby dependent on her for food and shelter, and he couldn't wait until spring!

She closed her eyes and a tremor ran through her. What was she going to do? Things had gotten progressively worse, it seemed, ever since she and her younger sister, Meg, had moved to Boise two years ago. They had been raised in a small Idaho town by an aunt, the spinster sister of their father, after their parents were killed in a plane crash. Aunt Liz had done what she called her duty, but she had begrudged every dime it took to feed and clothe her nieces. The two girls had lived for the day when Meg would be eighteen and Carrie nineteen, and they could leave their aunt's house and that dreary little town behind.

They had come to Boise with stars in their eyes. At first it had seemed that their dreams of a good life in the big city might be realized. They both found jobs in the office of a retail lumber company and moved into an attractive apartment. The lumber company was part of the huge Revell organization, which was headquartered in a town three hundred miles north of Boise near the Washington border in the heart of the vast forest lands owned and leased by the corporation.

Meg and Carrie had only been working at their new jobs two weeks when Danny Revell strolled in on one of his periodic visits to Revell businesses. It was a part of his duties as assistant to his older brother, Joshua Revell, the head of the corporation.

Danny Revell, she thought bitterly—the man who had changed the Franklin sisters' lives forever. On the day they met, Danny asked both Carrie and Meg to have dinner with him that evening. They accepted readily, since they knew few people in Boise.

At twenty-five Danny was tall, blond, and good-looking—the hail-fellow-well-met sort of man who always has a funny story to relate and always dressed with elegant style and frequented the finest places. But it had not taken Carrie long to realize that, underneath his surface charm, he was spoiled, selfish, and shallow. Meg, on the other hand, could see no flaw in him and within weeks was head over heels in love. The two began to date regularly whenever Danny was in town. On several occasions Carrie tried to caution her younger sister about letting herself become seriously involved with Danny. He was a member of one of the wealthiest families in the state, and Carrie doubted seriously that he wanted anything more than an occasional good time with her naïve little sister. But by that time Meg was too much in love to listen to reason.

Then had come that dreadful night when Meg had returned from a date with Danny and awakened Carrie, sobbing uncontrollably that she wanted to die. When Carrie got her calmed down, she discovered that Meg was pregnant with Danny's child. Upon learning the news earlier that evening, Danny had gone into a frenzy of rage, yelling that he would deny the child was his, that he wasn't fool enough to be trapped into a marriage he didn't want, and that he never wanted to see Meg again.

The next day Carrie had gone to Danny's hotel, hoping to find him in a more approachable frame of mind. She would never forget that confrontation as long as she lived.

"Do you think I would marry a small-town hick like your sister?" he had snarled at her. "Don't expect me to buy her off, either. I don't think that baby is mine!"

Carrie had been almost physically overwhelmed by the hate she saw in his blue eyes, and it had taken all her self-control not to slap his handsome, leering face. But something had warned her that Danny was on the edge of some emotional precipice, and she had clenched her hands into fists at her sides. "You know very well it's your baby!"

"Prove it!" he had cried, with a frightening triumph twisting his lips. "Now," he went on, "you listen to me. If you and your sister spread this story around, I'll make you regret it. Your reputations won't be worth mud when I get through, and you'll never get another job in Boise. Now, get out of here and don't ever come near me again!"

Fortunately, she had not told her sister that she intended to see Danny, so she did not have to tell her of his second rejection. Meg had stayed in the apartment for days, refusing to go out, refusing even to go to work for fear of running into him. A week later, however, Carrie learned from a co-worker that Danny Revell had been sent to South Africa to head one of the Revell businesses. It was all very unexpected and strange, Carrie's informant said; but Carrie thought bitterly that it was not strange at all. By removing himself from the country Danny was protecting himself against any charges Meg might be thinking of bringing.

About a month after that, the news had reached the lumber company that Danny had been killed in South Africa when his sports car had gone out of control and crashed.

Meg had returned to work until her pregnancy could no longer be disguised by loose jackets and sweaters. "What am I going to do?" she had wailed to Carrie on the morning that she discovered she could no longer get into any of her clothes. "We'll starve—but I can't go to Aunt Liz. Carrie, you must promise me you won't tell her. You know she never wanted us to come to Boise in the first place. She wanted us to stay in that awful town and pay her room and board."

She was becoming hysterical, and Carrie soothed her with assurances that sounded more heartfelt than they actually were. "We won't starve, honey, and we don't need Aunt Liz's help. We'll both resign our jobs at the lumber company. I'll say we've been called back home and that you've gone on ahead. I'll give a few weeks' notice—long enough to find another job. We'll manage, and we'll take care of the baby when it's born."

The next day Carrie had begun to carry out her plan. Several weeks later she found the job at the Simpson Car Agency. Meg stayed at home, took care of the apartment, and cooked their meals. Financially, it was an extremely tight three months while they waited for the baby's arrival.

The other problems that developed during those

three months proved to be worse than their financial condition, however. Meg fell into deep depressions that lasted for days, and then she began having kidney trouble. Her doctor tried numerous diets and medications, but the disease hung on all during the last two months of Meg's pregnancy, causing pain and even more severe depressions. The baby was born one cold January night, and twelve hours later Meg was dead from complications caused by her kidney disease.

In her last lucid moments, Meg had extracted a promise from Carrie that she would raise the baby. Later, Carrie realized that her sister had known she was going to die for some time, that she probably had wanted to die.

There was no longer any possibility of keeping the truth from Aunt Liz. Carrie had called to tell her of the baby's birth and Meg's death. Her aunt had grudgingly agreed to pay the funeral expenses, but she added that she hoped Carrie didn't expect her to help care for the child, since she was no longer physically or financially able to take on a burden like that. Not until that moment did Carrie realize she had been harboring a feeble hope that her aunt would insist on helping with the baby. But she only said that she and the baby would be fine, and then they had discussed shipping Meg's body back home for burial.

After the funeral Carrie took Mike back to the apartment she and her sister had shared. During the first two months, she didn't think she was going to make it. There was never enough money to last from one paycheck to the next, and the work involved in caring for an infant was unending. But Mike was healthy, a good baby, and he thrived under Carrie's sometimes awkward attempts to do what was best for him.

Then one day on the street Carrie ran into Janice Winton, a friend from high-school days. Jan, a willowy redhead, had moved to Boise immediately after graduation, searching for the bright lights and excitement that her daring, rather flamboyant nature craved. Carrie had always liked Jan, and on that blustery March afternoon the redhead had seemed like an angel sent straight from heaven. The meeting caught Carrie at a low point emotionally, and almost before she realized it she was sitting across from Jan in a restaurant pouring out everything that had happened to Meg and her since their arrival in Boise.

Wisely Jan let her talk, and when she was talked out the redhead said, "Oh, poor Meg, poor little kid. But, listen, I have a suggestion that might help you."

Jan had gone on to suggest that Carrie and Mike move into her apartment and share expenses. There was even a wonderful grandmotherly widow across the hall who, Jan assured her, would love caring for Mike while Carrie worked.

Things had been better after that. Living expenses were less, and, equally important, Carrie had someone to talk to in the evenings after she had put Mike to bed. She had even gone out several times with a friend she had met through Jan.

But now the capricious fate that had dogged her footsteps ever since she had come to Boise had stepped in again. . . .

Carrie shifted Mike to her left arm in order to take her key from her coat pocket and unlock the apartment door. She walked into the living room and crossed the gold shag carpet to the door of the bedroom that she shared with Mike. She had arrived at Mrs. Mawbrey's apartment before the widow had put Mike down for his afternoon nap. Now he was drowsy, his chubby little arms wound around Carrie's neck, his blond head resting on her shoulder. Standing beside his crib, she hugged him against her for a moment, feeling his drowsy warmth, inhaling the sweet baby smell of him.

Her happiest moments during the past ten months had been those spent with this child. Oh, how she loved him, with his short golden curls and blue eyes! She loved him with an ache that threatened to choke her at times. She could not have loved him more if she had given birth to him herself.

Gently she lowered him into the crib and pulled a soft blanket over his body. He gave a quiet little murmur, but his eyes remained closed, the brown lashes resting against the soft pink cheeks. Love for him welled up in Carrie anew, and she had to blink back tears. *We're going to make it, Mike,* she vowed silently.

Carrie was sitting on the couch in the shadowy living room when Jan arrived.

"Why are you sitting here in the dark?" Jan threw off her fake fur coat and walked through the apartment, turning on lights. Then, returning to the living room, she kicked off her high-heeled shoes and flopped into a chair. "Where's Mike?"

"Still napping."

"How did you make it home so early? I'm always here before you."

Carrie, wearing her heavy velour robe, was sitting sideways on the couch with her knees drawn up. She was hugging her legs as if she were chilled. "I left work early today."

Jan's green eyes contemplated her friend's pose with concern. "Not feeling well, huh? There's a lot of flu going around. Maybe you've caught a touch of it."

Carrie laid her forehead on her knees and said in a muffled voice, "No . . ."

Frowning, Jan got up and walked to the couch.

Looking down at the thick fall of hair that was hiding
Carrie's face, she touched a loose wave tentatively.
"You really do look pale, Carrie. Why don't you go to
bed, and I'll take care of Mike when he wakes up. I'll
make soup for dinner and call you when it's ready."
When Carrie did not reply, Jan sat down beside her.
"Can I bring you some aspirin or cold tablets—
anything?"

Carrie looked up then, and the unhappiness in her
blue-green eyes caused her friend to gasp. "Carrie,
what is it? You've been crying."

"I haven't got a cold or the flu, Jan. If I look ill it's
because I'm worried sick. I lost my job today."

Jan stared at her for a moment and then, recovering,
moved to put her arms around Carrie, pressing her
cheek against Carrie's hair. "Don't tell me you had a
fight with the boss?"

"No, nothing like that." Carrie's voice was weary.
"Actually, he said I'd done good work. But business is
bad and somebody had to go. Since I'd been there the
shortest time, I was chosen." She stirred, her stock-
inged feet sliding to the floor, her head falling back
against the couch. "I've been calling employment
agencies all afternoon. Nobody's hiring right now.
They all said to call back after the first of the year."

Jan sighed, getting to her feet to pace back and forth
across the living room. "Carrie, I'm sorry, but you
can't let it get you down like this. Something will come
along." She stopped in front of Carrie and thrust her
hands into the side pockets of her wool skirt. "Even if
you have to wait until the first of the year, it won't be
the end of the world."

"A couple of the agencies were looking for temporary evening clerks for department stores during the
Christmas shopping season. The hours are from five
until ten. But after I paid Mrs. Mawbrey for baby-
sitting, I doubt that I'd have much left."

Jan tossed her red hair back and resumed her restless pacing. "If you have to take one of those temporary jobs, I can watch Mike most evenings."

"Jan, you're a dear, but I can't expect you to take over my responsibilities with Mike. There's no reason for you to have to curtail your social life just because I lost my job."

"We'll get by," Jan said stoutly.

Carrie drew a long, unsteady breath. "It's time for Mike's checkup with the pediatrician, but I can put that off for a few weeks. I can't put off buying new shoes for him, though. His toes are touching the ends of the ones he's wearing now." She closed her eyes and said tiredly, "He deserves so much more than I can give him, Jan."

"What kind of talk is that?" Jan said indignantly. "Nobody could have taken better care of Mike. Certainly nobody could love him more than you do. Material things aren't important to children. You've been there for Mike, and I don't want to hear any more of that kind of talk from you!" When Carrie did not respond, Jan added, "We're going to work this out together. Trust me. I'll think of something." She was thoughtful for a moment. "I hear Mike waking up. You go get him, and I'll fix that soup."

A short while later Mike was sitting in his high chair between the two girls at the small kitchen table. Carrie fed him his soup first, then gave him a cracker to chew on while she ate her own dinner.

"I've been thinking," Jan said. "If Danny Revell was still alive, I'd say he ought to be forced to help you now. Since he isn't, I think you should call that big-shot brother of his and demand a financial settlement."

Carrie laid her spoon down and stared at her friend. Her face was so pale that her brows and thick lashes looked like smudges of stoveblack against her skin. "Joshua Revell is the last person on earth I'd go to for help!"

Carrie had seen Danny's older brother only once; he had joined her and Danny and Meg for dinner one evening when he was passing through Boise. But her memory of the powerful head of the Revell Corporation could still send a fearful tremor through her: that long, lean body, the almost savage hardness of it not at all camouflaged by the elegantly tailored dark blue suit he had worn; the thick, tiger-tawny hair that grew in deep sideburns down each side of his face; the brown eyes with the flecks of gold that had assessed Caroline boldly and clearly found her wanting; the stern-visaged face set in disapproving lines; the wide mouth, the upper lip ruthlessly hard, the lower lip fuller and somehow sensual.

Jan was looking at her impatiently. "But Mike's father was a Revell. As head of the family, Joshua Revell might want to help if he knew your situation. He's filthy rich. It's not as if he'd miss the money."

Not in a million years could Carrie imagine going to Joshua Revell and telling him that she was caring for his brother's illegitimate child, and that Meg had died as the result of what Danny had done to her. Even the thought of it tied Carrie's nerves in knots.

"No," Carrie said with vehemence. "We'll have to think of something else. And, please, don't mention that man to me again."

"Gosh, honey, I didn't mean to upset you," Jan said solicitously. "But don't you worry—about money, I mean. Leave that part to me."

"Of course I won't leave it to you." Carrie eyed her friend suspiciously. "But I won't go to Joshua Revell, and that's final."

"I'm not asking you to," Jan soothed. "Okay?"

After a moment Carrie nodded, picked up her spoon again, and began to eat. She was too lost in the maze of her own tangled thoughts to notice the calculating gleam that came into her friend's green eyes. Jan finished her soup and gazed past Carrie through the window into the gray November dusk.

During the next few days, Carrie checked out every lead she heard of for secretarial jobs. Every place she called had either recently hired someone or wanted to wait until after Christmas to break in a new employee. The only bright spot in her days was that she was able to spend more time with Mike, but even that was marred by the worry over money that remained at the back of her mind.

On Saturday morning she arose early to bathe and feed Mike. Then she settled him in his playpen with some toys while she cleaned the apartment. When Jan got up about eleven, Carrie left Mike with her to go to the supermarket for their weekly supply of groceries. The checkout lines were long, and after finally getting away she stopped at a shoe store that had infants' footwear on sale, where she found a pair the right size for Mike. It was after one when she got back to the apartment.

Jan appeared, having changed from her nightgown to jeans and a sweater. "I already fed Mike and put him down for his nap. I'll take these things to the kitchen, and then I'm going to run down to the drugstore. You better go into the living room. There's someone here to see you." She disappeared into the kitchen clutching two bags of groceries.

Carrie hung her coat in the foyer closet. Then, tugging her gold velour shirt down over the top of her brown corduroy jeans, she walked into the living room.

A tall man, at least six feet two inches, was standing at the window, his back to her. A muted tan and green plaid sports jacket molded itself to his broad shoulders, and his hands were thrust into the pockets of tan flannel trousers. In the first moment Carrie noticed that dark blond hair, which had a slight tendency to curl, overlapped the collar of his jacket in back.

Her heart began to pound erratically, for there was something vaguely familiar about this man. Apprehensively, she raked her slender fingers through her windblown hair. "Did you want to see me?"

He turned then, towering above her, dwarfing everything else in the room. His gold-flecked brown eyes narrowed as his gaze swept over her, disdain hardening the high cheekbones and deepening the noticeable cleft in his chin.

"Want, Miss Franklin?" Joshua Revell said. "No, I wouldn't say I *want* to see you. It seems I must."

Carrie's sudden lightheadedness forced her to catch hold of the back of the chair beside her to keep from falling. "Wh-what are *you* doing here?"

His tawny brows lifted sardonically. "I am here in answer to a phone call I received from your friend, Janice Winton, Thursday—as if you didn't know."

She shivered and sat down suddenly in the chair with which she had been supporting herself and took a shaky breath. She could feel Joshua Revell's cold gaze assessing her, reminding her acutely of that other time when she had felt gauche and hopelessly inadequate in his presence.

"Jan had no right to call you!" she said tensely. "So you could come here and look at me as if you think I—I—"

"As if I think you're a little schemer planning how you can get your hands on Revell money?" he murmured, and his glittering brown eyes looked directly down into hers, making her face flame with sudden overwhelming indignation. His look seemed to encompass her and strip her bare, and she caught her breath at what she saw in his eyes—icy contempt generously laced with ruthlessness.

"I knew that's what you—you would think!" Carrie's eyes blazed into his. "That's why I told Jan I wanted nothing to do with you. If I had known she intended to call you, I would have stopped her."

He stared down at Carrie's delicate-boned face, which was pale except for the dark brows and lashes and the dark smudges beneath her blue-green eyes. There was a quiver she could not control in her small chin, and her softly sculptured mouth and blazing eyes hinted at a passion she kept carefully buried beneath a coolly composed exterior.

This man's brother had plundered Meg's innate inviolateness, destroyed with hate the innocent purity which had been her sister's to give with love. As if that were not enough, he had destroyed Meg's life. Now Joshua Revell stood in her living room and devoured her with a look that stripped her of the remnants of her self-esteem, of the pride she had felt in living up to her promise to care for Meg's child.

"You feel so superior, don't you?" she cried. "You want to make me feel small and helpless. You are as cruel and heartless as your brother was!"

She sensed a rigid tightening of all the muscles of his body as he approached her with such deliberate intent that she shrank against the padded chair back.

"I did not come here to be insulted," he declared, "or to hear my late brother insulted, either. Danny is not here to defend himself, but I am. *Here,* I remind you, at the urgent request of your roommate. If—and I repeat, *if*—this baby you are caring for is Danny's child, he did not bring it into being alone. I do not wish to speak disrespectfully of the dead, but your sister was as much to blame as my brother in what happened, Miss Franklin."

She stared at him, unable for the moment to force any more words past the dry tightness in her throat. He must think that Meg had been some kind of playgirl, an amoral little featherbrain who jumped into bed with any man in sight. And if he thought that of Meg, he undoubtedly believed the same of Meg's sister.

"I don't think we have any more to say to each other," she said hoarsely.

The tensed muscles relaxed, and he stepped nonchalantly to the couch and sat down. "But we have," he said insolently. "I came here to satisfy myself as to the validity of your claims, and I intend to do just that."

"I have made no *claims* against you! I told you I didn't know my friend had phoned you, and I will not sit here and be called a liar and—worse."

Unruffled, he retorted, "Spare me the histrionics, please. I want answers to my questions."

"Wh-what questions?"

"How can I be sure that this baby is my brother's child?"

"Given your suspicions that everybody is out to get some of your money, you probably can't be," Carrie said with heavy sarcasm. "But I knew my sister. Meg was only eighteen and totally innocent when she met your brother. She was never with any other man, so there is not the slightest possibility that Mike's father could be anyone but Danny."

"Is Danny's name on the birth certificate as the father?"

"Yes," Carrie returned shortly, "although Mike goes by my sister's maiden name, Franklin. Your brother made it quite plain that he wanted nothing to do with the baby."

He eyed her dubiously. "Why would he do that if he knew the child was his?"

The disbelief in his tone cut across the space between them like a knife. "Well, *I* have a question for you, Mr. Revell. Why did Danny leave the country so suddenly?"

He shrugged. "I wouldn't say it was sudden, Miss

Franklin. We needed someone to oversee some copper mines we have acquired in South Africa. Danny volunteered for the job. He wanted to prove that he could handle the added responsibility."

"How convenient for him!" Carrie exclaimed. "That job gave him the chance to put several thousand miles between himself and the girl who was carrying his child. I think he was afraid Meg might decide to file a paternity suit against him."

He brushed her angry words aside. "Since Danny is dead, we will never know whether you are right, will we?" Then, in an abrupt change of subject: "Do you know the baby's blood type?"

"A-positive, but I don't see—"

His eyes narrowed. "The same as Danny's, as it happens, though I'm sure you know that doesn't prove anything."

She gripped the arms of her chair until her knuckles turned white. "I don't have to *prove* anything to you! How dare you—"

He cut her off rudely. "I would like to see the child now."

"He's asleep," she snapped.

He got to his feet. "Where? In here? I won't wake him." Before she could protest he had crossed the room and entered the bedroom. Several long minutes passed before he returned. He walked slowly to the couch and sat down.

"He has Danny's coloring," he mused, more to himself than to Carrie. After a pause, he looked up sharply. "I am still not convinced you are telling me the truth, however."

"Naturally," Carrie said bitterly. "You seem to hold such a low opinion of my sister and me, why should you believe me? You are very like your brother, Mr. Revell. He told me that he would deny paternity and that if we persisted in pressing Meg's claim he would see to it that neither of us ever worked in Boise again. The Revells are a charming family!"

His eyes narrowed warningly. "I must insist that you stop dishonoring my brother's name! Moreover, if I ever learn that you lied to me, about anything—"

"I do not lie!" Carrie's anger was so great that it was all she could do not to burst into furious tears.

Her reaction seemed of little concern to him. "I intend to investigate the matter further, Miss Franklin." He got to his feet with arrogant ease and strode toward the foyer. "You'll be hearing from me."

Before she could rush after him and cry that she never wanted to hear from him again, he had closed the door firmly behind him. Carrie stood in the foyer, trembling all over. How *dare* Joshua Revell come here and talk to her like that! And wait until she saw Jan!

She did not have long to wait. Apparently Jan had been watching from the drugstore downstairs for Joshua Revell to leave the building. She entered the living room, where Carrie was pacing back and forth, and said, "I hope you're not furious with me for calling him, but—"

"Well, I am!" Carrie retorted. "After I told you specifically that I wanted nothing to do with him!"

"Honey," Jan said coaxingly, "you do need his help. Mike deserves to gain some benefit from the fact that he is a Revell."

"Don't," said Carrie through clenched teeth, "say that name to me!"

During the next few days, Carrie lived in fear of hearing Joshua Revell's voice every time she answered the telephone or the door. But by Friday she had begun to doubt that he had ever really meant to get in touch with her again, and she began to feel calm.

Jan was planning to go on a skiing weekend with a

group of employees from the bank where she worked and had told Carrie Friday morning that she would probably be home early. So when the doorbell rang at two, Carrie assumed that her roommate had forgotten her key and ran to open the door before the chimes woke Mike from his nap.

"It's a good thing I'm here or—" Carrie's voice trailed away in midsentence as Joshua Revell stepped across the threshold. He was wearing khaki-colored denim trousers and a brown leather jacket over a gold turtleneck sweater, and he looked even more frightening than he had in coat and tie.

Carrie followed him into the living room, demanding, "I don't want you here. I have nothing to say to you. I want you to leave."

He turned to face her, a careless lock of tawny hair falling across his forehead, and his jaw set in determined lines. "I've had you and your sister investigated, Miss Franklin."

"You *what!*" Carrie felt the blood rush from her face. "You hired a private investigator?" She stomped across the room and gripped the back of a chair. "Who do you think you are? What right have you to be investigating us?"

He retorted coolly, "I had to know something about your character before I could decide whether or not I ought to believe your story."

"Get out!" Carrie fumed, gripping the chair back harder.

"No," he replied flatly and proceeded to seat himself on the couch. "It seems, Miss Franklin, that your sister was as innocent as you claim. Apparently she had dated no one but Danny since her arrival in Boise. As for you, you have been living an exemplary life since your arrival in town." She started to protest, but he waved her sputterings aside. "I've given this whole situation a great deal of thought this past week. If Mike is Danny's baby, I won't allow him to be raised in . . . these circumstances." He glanced about the simply furnished apartment disdainfully.

Carrie fought back a hysterical sob. "You will not allow it! *You* will not! Mr. Revell, you are not even entitled to an opinion in this matter!"

Before she even realized he had moved, he was standing beside her, gripping her shoulders, holding her roughly. He was so close to her that she could feel his warm maleness radiating in waves and the anger seething through his taut body. His hands tightened until they were hurting her, forcing a small gasp of pain from her lips.

"Don't!" Carrie jerked free, pushing at him until she had the chair between them again. "I've taken good care of Mike since I brought him home from the hospital when he was four days old. I'm sure this apartment doesn't compare with what you are accustomed to, but Mike has all that he needs. And I love him, which is more than you can say."

"So." Astounding as it seemed to Carrie, he looked curiously relieved. "There is that much in your favor, at least."

She forced a shaky laugh from her trembling body. "Is that supposed to make me feel better? Your good opinion may be important in some circles, but I assure you I couldn't care less what you think of me. I can do without your condescension, and I can certainly do without your money! After the way you've insulted me, I wouldn't take a dime from you if you begged me!"

Frowning, he thrust his hands into his trousers pockets and sauntered across the room, then turned to regard her steadily. "I was given to understand by your friend that you have lost your job and have no savings to carry you through until you find other employment. What *do* you intend to do?"

"I—I don't know yet. I'll find something, I'm sure. It doesn't take much for Mike and me."

He looked at her thoughtfully. "I am prepared now to admit that Mike is a Revell. As much as we may both dislike the idea, I feel a certain responsibility for him."

"I've already told you," she said, "I don't want your money."

"I did not come here to offer you money "

"Then why did you come, to gloat?"

His thick brows were drawn abruptly together into a dangerous frown, his eyes hard at the centers like glittering chips of gold. "My brother is no longer alive to assume his obligations, but his child must have the Revell name."

Carrie's heart was pounding like a trip-hammer. "What do you mean?"

He shrugged, but the tenseness of his stance revealed that he was not as relaxed as he wished to appear. "I would like to adopt Mike, Miss Franklin. I can offer him a good home, the best education . . "

"Everything money can buy!" she added derisively. "Well, you can stop right there. I have no intention of giving Mike up. I am the only mother he has ever known. I'm his whole world! Do you really imagine that the Revell name could take the place of that? Good Lord, you are arrogant!"

His eyes sparked gold fire as they held hers. "You have the tongue of a poisonous snake, Miss Franklin. But I don't want to waste my breath exchanging insults with you. I think you know any court in the state would decide that I can provide a much better home for Mike than you can."

"You can't do this! I'll leave Boise. I'll take Mike so far away from Idaho that you will never find us!"

"Don't make foolish threats." He moved around the chair to stand in front of her, his eyes still on her face. "With enough money to pay investigators, you could be found. And I have enough money." He watched as her hand came up to cover her eyes for a moment. Then he said, "There is one other choice open to you."

Mutely, she stared into his face.

"You can marry me," he went on deliberately. "We can get the license Monday and we should be able to marry on Wednesday."

Carrie was at a loss for words. She could only gaze at Joshua Revell in dumb astonishment, until abruptly her body shook with a shrill, humorless laugh. "Marry?" she exclaimed. "You? Do you think I'd marry a total stranger who obviously considers me some kind of low-life? I'd rather die!"

"Are you always so melodramatic?" he inquired calmly. "Sorry to disappoint you, but I am not moved by such threats. I have made up my mind, and it does seem to me that marriage is the best way out of your present situation."

"I can't believe you are actually serious!"

"But I am—quite serious."

"The very thought of what your brother did to my sister makes me sick," she said fiercely. "And I despise you for coming in here with your insults and your threats. I may be in dire straits, but I still have some pride left."

He stopped her near-hysterical tirade by pressing a hand over her mouth. "Listen to me! Regardless of what you thought of my brother, Mike has a right to his father's name and all that goes with it. That little boy in there *will* be raised as a Revell—one way or another. Do I make myself clear, Miss Franklin?"

His hand dropped carelessly to her shoulder, where it lay heavy and warm through the velour of her shirt. For a fleeting instant she thought she saw something human—compassion, perhaps—in his eyes. But then it was gone, banished behind the shade that came down and turned his face into a stone mask.

"Try to get hold of yourself and consider this calmly. Think about the alternatives. Even if you can manage financially until you find another job, you can't afford to fight me in court. And think about the baby. Do you really want to raise an illegitimate child? Consider how that could affect him when he's old enough to understand."

She twisted away from his grip and buried her face in her hands, struggling to remain calm, to think clearly.

"The only other choice is to marry me," he went on relentlessly, his harsh words hammering at her, peeling away whatever illusions she might have had about finding a happier solution.

Carrie lifted her head and gazed into his eyes, so astonishingly golden and luminous in the poorly lighted room. Wind-tanned skin, thick dark blond hair, lashes the color of dark chocolate at the base and curving upward into a honey color at the tips. She had never seen such a striking man; she would surely have admired his utterly masculine good looks if he had been anyone other than who he was. But in his veins ran the same blood as that of the man who had ripped apart her sister's innocence and destroyed her life, and Carrie hated him for that.

"I couldn't live like that, playacting at a farce of a marriage," she said. "You don't seem to understand that I hate the name Revell."

A muscle in his jaw jerked as she spat the words at him. The hard bones of his face seemed to protrude even further and the dark centers of his eyes expanded with molten fire. He looked as if he wanted to shake her. Carrie felt a small flicker of triumph that she had managed to puncture his ego, however briefly.

"After I have legally adopted Mike and he has had enough time to come to think of me as his father—if you still feel the same way—you can have a divorce and a financial settlement substantial enough to allow you to live the rest of your life in more comfortable circumstances than you have enjoyed up till now."

"I—I have to think," she said rather faintly. "This whole idea is preposterous, and yet—"

"And yet," he finished curtly, "you really have no viable alternative. You will agree because it is by far the best solution to your problem."

"W-would Mike and I have to live in your house?"

"Of course. I must insist upon that. My house is very large, however, so perhaps you could manage to avoid running into me often." The taunt in his words was palpable. "We must present a united front to the world, for Mike's sake."

Carrie could feel the furious protest clamoring at her lips. But apart from the fact that his reasoning made perfect sense, there was in Joshua Revell's eyes a look that warned her he was not willing to tolerate any more insults. It was plain to Carrie that he meant to have his way, and he was a man with enough power and influence to get his way in almost any matter. She might refuse to marry him, but she was certain that if she did he would take Mike away from her.

"There are two stipulations I will make." He gazed directly into her eyes, making it impossible for her to look away. "First, no one else is to know that Mike is Danny's child."

"But Jan—"

"I am certain your friend's silence can be assured." A mocking smile played at one corner of his mouth. "She seems an eminently practical young woman—far more than you, I must say."

"What is the second stipulation?"

"If you ever decide to leave, Mike will stay with me. I will have custody."

Carrie managed to brush aside the tremor of unease that she felt. Strange as it seemed, Joshua Revell appeared already to have developed a feeling for Mike as a member of the proud Revell family. He had certainly left her in no doubt that what he was doing was for the child's sake. He was willing to provide for her and give the child his name, making no further demands except that he wanted Mike to grow up a part of a respected, influential family. And no matter how she despised the knowledge, Mike *was* a Revell.

Suddenly all her arguments against his plan seemed flimsy, and the fight drained out of her. "All right." She gave a helpless shrug. "I'll agree to your conditions. As long as we're going through with this charade, I'd like to have the wedding with as little fuss and ceremony as possible."

"I quite agree," he returned mockingly. "I know a judge here. We'll go to his chambers. No one else need be present except for the witnesses. I'll ask a friend to stand up with me, and perhaps you would like to ask Miss Winton."

She nodded dumbly.

"I'll take care of the arrangements," he said with a sudden brusqueness, as if he were concluding a minor business deal. "I'll call for you on Monday and we'll get the license."

"Very well, Mr. Revell," she agreed dispiritedly.

"Now that we are engaged," he said dryly, "you'd better get used to calling me Josh. What do your friends call you—Caroline?"

"Carrie."

"Goodbye for now, Carrie. Until Monday." He strode from the room, and Carrie, discovering that her knees had turned to rubber, lowered herself to the couch.

She was still sitting there a few minutes later when Jan breezed into the apartment. "Gotta rush. Mind if I borrow your down jacket? Carrie, honey, whatever is wrong? You look as if you've seen a ghost."

Carrie looked up at her friend, who stood in the

center of the room, a great deal of puzzlement in her green eyes.

"I am going to marry Joshua Revell," Carrie heard herself say in even tones. But inwardly she was quaking, the stunning realization of what she had agreed to do belatedly penetrating her dazed consciousness with full force.

Chapter Two

The table that was waiting for them at the hotel where Josh had been staying in Boise was in a private alcove, one of several off the main dining room. It was already set for two, and a bucket on another small table alongside held ice and a bottle of champagne.

Carrie noticed how the young waitress kept glancing at Josh as she took their order. No doubt Joshua Revell was a valued guest, but Carrie felt that the waitress was a little too eager to please. She didn't doubt that the girl was envying her and would have given almost anything to change places with her.

She couldn't fail to see the irony in the situation. She and Josh, married little more than an hour, were anything but typical newlyweds. It seemed almost impossible that the waitress couldn't sense the strangeness in their relationship. They weren't touching hands across the table or gazing into each other's eyes as if they couldn't wait to be alone together. And Carrie kept her left hand in her lap, concealing the wide platinum band set with four large diamonds that Josh had placed on her slender finger in the judge's chambers. She had been shocked at its price tag when Josh had picked it out for her the day before and had tried to steer him toward the plain gold bands. He had smiled sardonically when the jeweler remarked that a beautiful woman like Carrie deserved diamonds.

"After all, miss," the jeweler had said to Carrie, "you will only marry once."

"You sound awfully sure of that." Carrie couldn't resist the opportunity to needle Josh a little.

The jeweler had been slightly flustered. "Why, I am. I can tell by looking at you and Mr. Revell that you are very much in love."

"Don't tease him, my dear," Josh had said dryly. "He's had enough experience to be a good judge in these matters."

"Was that really necessary?" Carrie had asked when they had left the store. "Pretending that we're madly in love."

"Of course, Carrie." He had looked down at her with an unreadable expression. "We are going to be married. You really must learn to play your part more convincingly."

"That won't be easy," she said grimly. "I never imagined marrying for anything but love." Relenting a little, she added, "But then I don't suppose you expected your marriage to be a fake, either—after escaping the matrimonial state for so long, too."

"Our marriage, whatever else it may be, will not be a fake. When we leave the judge's chambers tomorrow, legally we will be man and wife."

"I didn't mean—oh, you know what I meant."

"Yes, Carrie, I think I do." His sideways glance made her feel oddly uncomfortable. He cupped his hand under her elbow to steer her across the street.

"Also, you seem to have drawn a false conclusion. This won't be my first marriage."

That unexpected bit of information caused her to look up at him with surprise. Curious, she had wanted to ask more. Was he divorced—or widowed? If he'd had children by that other marriage, surely he would have mentioned it. But he had such a closed look on his face, all at once, that she hadn't the courage to question him.

Already she sensed that he was a private sort of person. Sitting across the table from him, she wondered what he was thinking. There was no denying that he looked suave and stylish in his three-piece brown suit with shirt and tie in cream and brown, wearing the shining gold band that he had provided for her to place on his marriage finger.

An observer could easily guess that he was successful in business and probably a member of an influential family. At thirty-five (Carrie had gleaned that fact when they had applied for the marriage license and were asked their ages) he was in the prime of life, both physically and professionally.

"Are you divorced?" she suddenly asked him.

He looked at her a trifle amused, for she had been silent ever since they had left the judge's chambers as husband and wife. She had been angered at the unexpected kiss he had dropped at the corner of her mouth, even though she knew it was only for show in front of the best man and the judge, both friends of Josh.

"My wife died five years ago. We were married for three years."

"I'm sorry." She looked into his face, and her eyes against the background of her powder-blue suit and ivory silk blouse, took on the color of a summer sky.

"Why should you be? It's nothing to do with you."

He fell silent, his brown eyes fixed broodingly upon the champagne glass in his hand.

"It's just that I've been so caught up in what I was feeling that I didn't stop to think about you. After being happily married, this must be doubly awkward for you."

He swirled the liquid in the bottom of his glass. "I assure you, Carrie, I have few illusions about marriage."

It had taken a lot of courage for her to make a friendly overture, and his seeming rebuff caused her to feel fresh resentment. "Well, I had—not illusions, but dreams. But that doesn't seem to concern you. You don't care that the Revells destroyed my sister, not to mention me."

"Carrie, if you are destroyed, no one would ever guess it by looking at you." His eyes were narrowed and slightly mocking as they wandered over the loose falling waves of her hair and the creamy delicacy of her face, settling for a moment on her soft, rosy mouth. "You look very beautiful."

"You can thank yourself for that. Your money bought everything I am wearing." Two days ago he had given her more money than she had ever made in an entire month and ordered her to spend it all on a wedding outfit. "Of course, I realize I have to look my best if I'm to be seen with a Revell."

He chose to ignore the sneer in her words. "We do make a good-looking couple, don't we? Heads turned when we walked through the dining room together."

"What an egotistical thing to say!" Her cool blue eyes studied his face, seeing the ruthlessness in the hard angle of cheekbone and chin, a suggestion of sensuality in the firmly sculptured mouth.

"I never claimed to be the humble sort. That's not my style." He said it tauntingly.

"No, I'm sure it isn't."

Something in the unwavering gaze of the gold-flecked eyes hinted at a deep well of passion, a suggestion that he knew all the ways to arouse a woman's darkest desires. What *would* it be like to be held in Joshua Revell's arms? The direction of Carrie's wayward thoughts shocked her, causing her to blush; at the unbidden awareness of Joshua Revell as the epitome of masculinity, a sudden alarming anxiety passed through her.

This man who was looking at her with such calculating perusal was her husband! The rings they wore, the promises they had made in the judge's chambers, bound them to each other with mutual rights and privileges. But theirs was a marriage in name only—they both understood that. There had never been a suggestion of anything else. Yet, looking at him across the table, she was suddenly very aware of the strength of his will. Hadn't he forced her into this marriage? Nothing would deter him if he should decide to claim her body.

"I wasn't referring to your clothes when I said you were beautiful," he murmured now. "You have the face of an angel—although your sharp tongue rather tarnishes the image." There was a wicked twinkle in his eyes.

Carrie felt a tormenting flush of uneasiness. "Does it give you any satisfaction that the wife who has been forced upon you will, at least, not injure your pride by her appearance? I suppose it would have been a terrible embarrassment if the woman who had your brother's child had turned out to be an ugly witch." Her tone was cool, like her eyes, but her mind was remembering how his warm lips had felt in that brief moment when they had brushed across her mouth.

He laughed softly. "I do not purposely put myself in embarrassing situations. Nor are things forced upon me. I don't do anything I don't want to do, Carrie."

She was saved from replying to that enigmatic statement by the waitress, who arrived at that moment with their lunch.

"You haven't drunk your champagne," Josh said quietly as the waitress left. "This is an occasion for celebrating."

She picked up her glass and lifted it to her lips, allowing her dark lashes to shadow her eyes.

Josh raised his glass to her with a mocking smile. "To Mr. and Mrs. Joshua Revell. What? Don't you want to drink to that?"

"I can't be as callous as you are. Or is this your way of trying to hurt me?"

"Come, my dear, don't tell me my wife has no sense of humor."

"I'm afraid I can't find anything humorous in our situation, Josh. And don't call me your dear. There's no one around to hear you now."

"Lower your voice," he said in a pleasant tone, but there was a warning in his eyes. "I wouldn't like everyone in the hotel to hear us quarreling so soon after the wedding."

"I don't care! I—I resent being here with you. I want to see Mike. Where has that shrewish old woman taken him?"

He had become very still, like a wild animal poised before attack. "You are spoiling our first meal together. Our plane leaves in an hour." Deliberately he cut into the chicken breast on his plate. "That shrewish old woman, as you call her, is a competent nurse on the hotel staff. She is giving Mike his lunch and will bring him to us in the lobby in a few minutes. Now, eat your meal."

"Yes, master," she said with sarcasm. "Is this how you treated your first wife, ordering her around like a servant? Well, I don't have to take it, Josh. As soon as

Mike has the precious Revell name, I can take him and leave you any time."

"Don't push me too far, my beautiful wife." As he continued to look at her, goose bumps rose on her arms. "You will not leave me, Carrie, unless and until I allow it. If you try, I will find you and bring you back."

"Oh, stop tormenting me!" She fumbled for the napkin beside her plate and held it to her eyes, turning her face away from him to gaze blindly at the rich deep red of the carpet. How was she to bear living in the same house with this man?

He was silent for some moments as he ate a few bites of his meal. Finally, he put down his fork. "We must leave in a few minutes." He reached across the table and touched the fingers of her free hand which lay limply beside her plate. "You had better eat something."

"I don't feel like eating," she said wearily, pulling free of his touch.

"Carrie, these infantile tantrums of yours are quite ridiculous. Don't you think it's time you began to think about Mike and what's best for him instead of feeling sorry for yourself? You agreed to marry me, so grow up and try to make the best of it."

"It's because I was thinking of Mike that I am here now, but you can't expect me to like it. You make it sound so easy, to make the best of things." She dropped the napkin, and her eyes bore into his. "You are going back to your home, and you have managed to get Mike. But I—I know I'm going to hate it!"

"It doesn't have to be that way," he said with impatient curtness. "There is no reason why this marriage couldn't be very pleasant for you. You will have a good home and standing in society. You will have money for whatever you wish to buy. You aren't a prisoner."

A shudder went through her. "But I am, Josh, in a way. I love Mike too much to be separated from him. You have made it clear that you mean to keep him with you. Is it any wonder I think of your house as a prison?"

"You're exaggerating, my dear," he said sarcastically. "We make our own prisons with our attitudes. You must begin to look at the positive aspects of being my wife."

"Mrs. Revell," she said coldly.

He gave a soft laugh. "You may find yourself adjusting quite well to being a Revell before we're through." He tossed a bill on the table. "I find I'm not hungry, either. It's time we got Mike and left for the airport."

They made it to the terminal with only a few minutes to spare. Josh checked their luggage through, then, holding Mike in one arm, grabbed Carrie's hand and pulled her after him toward the gate.

When they were buckled into their seats, the runway falling away below them, Mike gurgled happily on Josh's lap, exploring his pockets mischievously until Josh gave him a large ring of keys to play with. The child laid his blond head against Josh's shoulder contentedly and examined the keys, one by one.

Carrie pushed down the resentment she was feeling at the way her husband had taken over Mike for the flight. After a moment she asked, "Do you live alone?"

"My mother lives with me. She has a slight heart condition and is a semi-invalid, keeping to her own suite of rooms much of the time. I hope you and Mother will be friends. She enjoys company, and while I try to visit her every day, I can never stay long enough to satisfy her. I would appreciate it if you would spend time with her on a regular basis."

The information that he looked after his mother did

WONDER AND WILD DESIRE 43

not surprise Carrie. The importance he had placed on Mike's Revell blood proved that he put a high priority on his family. "Your father is dead, then?"

He nodded. "For ten years now. He died when his private plane crashed. That's when I took over as head of the corporation. His death was so unexpected that I wasn't really prepared to step into his shoes."

"I am sure you managed very well," she murmured. "I think you are a man who could cope with anything life handed him."

His brown eyes swept over her, taking in the creamy curve of her neck where the silk blouse was opened slightly. "You are an experienced judge of men, no doubt," he said with a soft laugh.

"Not really," Carrie said coldly. She met his gaze steadily. "But I think I know stubbornness and ruthlessness when I see them."

"Meaning that those are my outstanding qualities?" He raised an eyebrow. "Nevertheless, I worked night and day for the first two years after my father died before I really felt I had a good rein on things." His expression changed to one of speculation. After a pause, he said, "I know things have not turned out as you might have fantasized in your adolescent dreams. But there was certainly no need for you to struggle as you have since Mike's birth. I cannot understand why you didn't ask for my help months ago."

"That thought never crossed my mind," she said, astonishment showing on her face. "Your brother reacted to the news with selfish cruelty. After he died I just assumed you would not believe me if I came to you claiming that Mike was Danny's child. Besides, the one time I saw you two years ago, it was obvious you didn't think very highly of me."

He twisted around in his seat and was staring at her. "Why do you say that?"

Carrie was alarmed by the sudden alertness in his

eyes. "It—it was the way you looked at me, as if I were beneath your notice."

With a sudden movement he captured her left hand in his. "What a tragic imagination you have, Carrie. As I recall, I'd been in meetings all day and was extremely tired that evening." His fingers pressed the new wedding ring into her flesh, hurting her a little. When she winced, he relaxed his grip, as if he had just realized what he was doing, and released her hand, which she clutched into a small fist in her lap.

"You are not to tell my mother anything about your sister and Danny," he said abruptly. "She mustn't know that Danny refused to acknowledge his child, or that you refused to let the family know of Mike's existence. She would resent you for that, I'm afraid, and a friendship between the two of you would be difficult."

"Resent *me!*" she said fiercely. "If you and your mother knew the half of what Meg went through—"

His eyes narrowed. "I know your sister suffered. But I cannot condone the way you behaved after her death, without even giving us a chance to help you. It somehow smacks of a martyr complex, Carrie."

She made a sound that was half sob, half bitter laugh. Josh looked at her curiously. "I realize you were judging all the Revells by what you saw of my brother. Danny was headstrong, and he had been spoiled. He was only fifteen when our father died, and since I had to take over the business and had little time at home, Mother had full charge of him. Unfortunately, he learned very quickly how to get around her. Because she had lost Dad, she tended to smother Danny. He rebelled and ran a little wild for a while. But after he came to work for me, he seemed to settle down. I thought he was starting to grow up at last."

Mike had fallen asleep, and Josh shifted the child to a

more comfortable position in his arms. Carrie bent forward, pressing her hands against her forehead in a gesture of infinite weariness.

"Why are you looking like that?" Josh asked with ill-concealed impatience. "What are you thinking?"

Carrie threw her head up, tilting her chin. "I am thinking that you had remarkably poor insight where your brother was concerned."

All at once he was scowling, his face unyielding. "My mother worshiped the ground Danny walked on. I will not have her disillusioned. You are never to utter an unkind word about my brother in her presence. Is that clear?"

"Yes," she whispered as he continued to stare at her.

"Good," he retorted and leaned back against the seat, eyes closed.

All of Carrie's being burned with resentment toward the man beside her—her husband. She despised herself for sitting there silently and taking his abuse. She put her head back and closed her eyes, feeling such hopeless desperation that she wanted to die. How had her life become so complicated in such a short time? How was she to go into Joshua Revell's house and face his mother and pretend to be an adoring wife? Her financial worries might be over, but she was beginning to realize that other, perhaps even worse problems had replaced them.

Neither of them spoke again until the plane had landed. Josh settled Mike, who was awake again, on the seat long enough to reach up for Carrie's white wool coat and help her into it.

"Will anyone be meeting us?" she asked.

He shook his head. "My car's in the airport parking lot. It's not a long drive."

She put Mike's coat and cap on him and Josh carried him from the plane. She brushed aside his suggestion that she and Mike wait in the terminal until he could bring the car around and, hugging the baby against her body, accompanied Josh to the parking lot.

The late afternoon was already gray with dusk. The days were growing shorter, and as Carrie saw the shadows of the mountains that surrounded this valley on all sides, she could easily visualize them covered with snow as they would be in a few weeks' time. As winter shrouded everything with ice and snow the valley might seem a protected haven to some, but it could be a prison to one who had no wish to be there. Carrie shivered at the thought and was glad when they reached Josh's car, a silver-gray Mercedes.

The lumber town was soon left behind and she listened to the powerful, purring motor of the Mercedes as it climbed the lower slope of the mountain. She settled Mike on the seat between them. The little boy's blue eyes were wide as he gazed at the interior of the unfamiliar car.

"My house is about five miles from town," Josh told her. "I hope you won't mind having no close neighbors."

"It doesn't matter," she murmured tiredly.

"I'll arrange for you to have a car, of course, so that you can feel free to leave the house when you wish."

As long as she didn't go too far, Carrie thought morosely. But she did not reply, having no heart either to argue with him or to thank him for what, on the surface, seemed to be consideration for her happiness. Knowing that she would have a car at her disposal did little to lighten her depression at being here in an unfamiliar place among strangers.

"What have you told your mother about me?"

"Only that we have known each other for some time—which is true, in a way. And that you've been raising your sister's child, whom I intend to adopt." His glancing perusal was thoughtful. "My mother is usually very tactful, so I doubt that she will question you about Mike's father. If she does, I'm sure you can satisfy her without revealing the truth. When I spoke to her on the phone she was very happy about the prospect of being a grandmother."

He turned the car into a formidable entrance with stone pillars on either side and they approached a rambling house of stone and dark-stained redwood with a wide, wrought-iron columned porch across the front. The center section of the house was two stories, with single-story wings angling out from it. Even knowing that Josh was wealthy hadn't fully prepared her for the imposing size of it. Although it was now almost too dark to see much of the grounds, Carrie could tell they covered several acres.

"It's beautiful," she said as Josh parked the car in an attached garage tucked behind one wing of the house.

"A good place for a child to grow up," Josh agreed. He took Mike and they entered the house through a door at the back of the garage which led into a small entryway.

Josh hung their coats in a hall closet. Then, perhaps sensing her nervousness, he placed his free arm around her shoulders and drew her through a large formal dining room into a cozy sitting room where a fire burned in a stone fireplace.

A tall, slender, gray-haired woman sat in a wing-backed chair near the fire with a half-finished knitted afghan in her lap. As they entered she looked up expectantly and smiled. Josh led Carrie to her chair and bent to kiss the woman's pale cheek. She took his hand and patted it fondly. "Josh, this has been the longest day of my life! I thought you'd never get here!" Now she was smiling at Carrie.

With one hand still on Carrie's shoulder, Josh gave

every appearance of being a loving husband. What an actor he was! "Mother, this is my wife, Carrie. And this handsome fellow is Mike."

Carrie stepped forward and took the slender, cool hand offered to her. "How do you do, Mrs. Revell."

Josh's mother clicked her tongue against her teeth. "Now, we'll have none of that. My name is Ethel, but I'd really like it if you would call me Mother. Welcome to our home, Carrie—your home now." She turned her smile on Mike, who, with an uncharacteristic attack of shyness, had tucked his head under Josh's chin. "Yours, too, Mike. Oh, Carrie, he is adorable."

Carrie smiled as warmly as she could. "Thank you—Mother."

Ethel Revell tucked her knitting into a large sewing bag beside her chair. "Sit down, my dear. I know you're tired after your trip."

Gratefully Carrie sat on the loveseat that faced the wingbacked chair with a large oval braided rug between them. Josh put Mike down on the rug, and the baby immediately crawled to the loveseat and pulled himself up to press against Carrie's legs. She caressed his golden curls, realizing that he was feeling a little frightened by the strange surroundings.

"I imagine you ate before leaving Boise," Ethel Revell said, "but I asked Betty to prepare a tray of sandwiches, petits fours, and tea for us. Josh, would you mind finding her and asking her to bring it in?"

While Josh was gone his mother questioned Carrie about her home and family, expressing sympathy over her sister's untimely death and saying how admirable it was of Carrie to have taken on the care of her sister's child. The meeting Carrie had dreaded didn't turn out to be so difficult after all. Ethel Revell did not ask about Mike's father, perhaps sensing that this was a sensitive topic. She seemed to want to put Carrie at ease, but Carrie couldn't help thinking how shocked this sweet, gray-haired woman would be if she knew that Mike was Danny's child.

After they had had their tea and talked for a while, the older woman excused herself to go to her apartment at a far end of the ground floor, saying that she knew Carrie would like a chance to see her own quarters and get Mike settled after the flight. Carrie winced inwardly at the unexpressed but obvious sensitivity of Josh's mother, who naturally thought the newlyweds would want to be alone.

When they were alone, Josh said, "Come, I'll show you your room—and Mike's. Adam Carney, the groundskeeper and handyman, our housekeeper's husband, has already taken our bags up. Betty told me that Mother has acquired a crib, playpen, and high chair for Mike." He lifted the baby into his arms and went ahead of Carrie up the stairs.

On the second floor, he opened the first door in the hallway to the left of the landing and stood aside so that Carrie could precede him into the room. The bedroom was large, its walls papered with soft blue flowers against a white background. The carpet was thick and also a soft blue. The furniture was French provincial in styling, white with gold trim. The draperies at the wide windows were white antique satin. The undercurtains a pale, glistening gold.

Josh walked across the bedroom and opened a door, gesturing for her to come and look at the most luxurious bath she had ever laid eyes on. There was an enormous sunken tub in the center of the room. It had gold fixtures and a white satin shower curtain on a circular track which surrounded the tub completely. A long vanity ran along a wall with one large mirror over it, and the floor was covered with thick white carpeting.

"What do you think of it?"

Too aware of his closeness behind her, Carrie turned and ducked under his arm to return to the bedroom. "It's much finer than anything I've ever seen. I feel out of place in such elegant surroundings."

"You'll get used to it," said Josh. He walked back across the bedroom to double louvered doors. "This is a dressing room which Mother has converted into a room for Mike—for the time being." Carrie followed him into the small room, where a new crib stood against one wall with several toys and stuffed animals in it.

"Well, Mike." Josh set the little boy in the crib and offered him a small fuzzy bear. "Teddy has been waiting for you." Mike grabbed the bear in both hands and squealed happily.

Josh laughed and turned to Carrie. "He's going to adjust very well, I think." He returned to the bedroom and walked to another door in the wall opposite the bath. "This leads into my suite." He put his hand on the knob but did not open the door.

"Is—is there a key?" Carrie asked.

His look was mocking. "This door will never be locked, Carrie. We wouldn't want the servants to get the wrong idea, would we?"

"Don't you mean the right idea?" Carrie said in her coolest tone of voice. Another squeal of delight came from beyond the louvered doors where Mike had evidently discovered another new toy. She turned away from Josh and took off her suit jacket, tossing it on the blue satin bedspread. Although she hadn't heard him move—the thick carpeting muffled footsteps—she was suddenly aware of his closeness and whirled about to stare up into his face.

Strong hands gripped her upper arms, heat penetrating from them through the silk of her blouse. "Is that your way of telling me that you intend to make our relationship platonic?"

Her heart hammered in her chest as she became

aware of the dangerous light in his eyes. "You—you know that was our agreement."

His gaze roamed over her hair and face. "I remember no such agreement, Carrie. I don't recall that the subject was ever mentioned, actually."

"But you c-can't mean to—" She found that she was quite breathless. "W-we hardly know each other!"

"What better way to become acquainted, my beautiful wife?" Suddenly she was gathered against him and, before she knew what was happening or could think what to do about it, his lips had captured hers with such a warm provocative exploration that she lost her breath. It was a long, demanding kiss, his lips crushing, possessing, the intimacy increasing as his tongue found hers.

Carrie felt as if her body were welded to his, and her mouth was softening, melting, becoming one with his mouth. A swooning sort of feeling had invaded her body, weakening her, making her feel that she would surely faint any second.

Then he lifted his head and, still holding her against him, murmured huskily, "You are my wife, Carrie. We are one in the eyes of God and the state, whether you wish to accept it or not."

"I married you only because you forced me to, and you know it." Her voice sounded strangely weak.

"Nevertheless, can't we enjoy our situation?"

She tried to twist away from him, but he held her fast. "Enjoy!" she gasped. "Do you think I could enjoy having a Revell pawing over me?"

He stared down at her, a muscle in his jaw twitching slightly. "I promise you," he drawled, "I could teach you to enjoy it."

"I hate you!" she spat at him. "You brought me here under false pretenses! Well, anything you get from me you will take by force!" She might have said more, but the look in his flashing eyes stopped her.

"We'll see about that!" He spoke through gritted teeth. "Do you really think you can live like a nun indefinitely, with only an unlocked door separating you from your husband?"

Josh let her go abruptly and, turning on one heel, walked toward his suite. He did not look back as he closed the door firmly behind him.

Chapter Three

Carrie walked about the spacious room, her anxiety over her husband's unexpected behavior gradually giving way to a grudging admiration for her surroundings. She trailed her fingers over the satiny finish of the dressing table and a large armoire, stopping to stare down at the oversized satin-covered bed, both hands on one tall carved post of the footboard.

This must have been Josh's first wife's room. How could he help but think of her whenever he came here? Had she looked anything like Carrie? The idea came as something of a shock to Carrie. It was the first time she had really wondered about that first wife—how she had looked, what sort of woman she had been. It occurred to her that if she, Carrie, resembled the other woman in some way, that might explain Josh's suggestion that they marry. In which case there might be a little more to the marriage, in her husband's mind, than simply his desire to raise his brother's son. This possibility caused her to shiver uncomfortably. If Josh had married her because she reminded him of his first wife, he was heading for a big letdown. She was, she told herself, nothing like any woman who could have fallen in love with Joshua Revell, even a younger Joshua Revell who had probably been less arrogant and ruthless than the man Carrie had married.

She walked over to the large closet and opened louvered doors, half expecting to see the first wife's clothes still hanging there, but the closet was completely bare. Relieved, Carrie put her suitcases on the bed and began to arrange her clothes in the closet and the armoire. When she had finished, she carried Mike's things into the adjoining dressing room and placed them in the drawers of the chest. The baby was lying on his side, playing drowsily with the Teddy bear. His big blue eyes followed her to the chest. He sat up with a gurgle of laughter and held his arms out to her.

"Mama!" he squealed.

Carrie found a disposable diaper and changed him. "You've missed your nap, little man," she cooed to him. "Too much going on today, I expect." She finished pinning the diaper and pulled his corduroy rompers down over his chubby legs again, securing the snap closing. "Come on. We'll both lie down for a rest."

She lifted him and carried him to her own bed. Pulling back the covers, she set him down in the center of the bed and slipped out of her skirt and blouse, crawling under the sheet and satin coverlet with him.

Looking down at his tousled blond curls and soft, vulnerable features, Carrie felt the familiar warm flood of love for him. Oh, Mike, she said silently, have I done the right thing bringing you here? Everything was so different that it must be confusing to a small child. But *she* was still with him; she was Mike's anchor in this new, perhaps frightening environment. Never, no matter what happened between her and Josh, would she allow herself to be separated from this child. She curled her legs up around his baby warmth and drifted into a dreamless sleep.

When she awakened, the room was gloomy with dark evening shadows. Yawning, she let her glance slide over the bed and discovered that the baby was no longer there. Had he fallen out? But surely, if that had happened, he would have cried and awakened her. Nevertheless, she got out of bed and walked around it; but there was no sign of Mike.

She checked his crib and found it empty, also, except for the toys. A quick, furtive glance into Josh's suite revealed it to be unoccupied at the moment, as well. Feeling a slight flicker of worry, she wondered if Josh had taken Mike downstairs. Turning on one of the dressing-table lamps, she saw propped against the lamp base a note addressed to her in a heavy masculine scrawl.

Carrie,
I've gone to the office to go through my mail. You and Mike were sleeping so peacefully, it seemed as good a time as any. I shouldn't be too late.

Josh

So Josh had come into the room while she and Mike slept. She glanced down at the sheer lacy bra and half-slip that she wore and felt her face growing warm as she wondered how well covered she had been when Josh was in the room, standing beside the bed looking down at her and the baby.

She went to the closet, found a pair of jeans and a long-sleeved cotton chambray shirt, and put them on, then stepped into crepe-soled loafers. One question had been answered, at least. Mike was not with Josh. She hurried down the stairs, puzzled who had taken him, for she didn't think a baby could descend the stairs on his own, and if he had fallen, the whole house would have heard his cries.

Her concern was allayed almost at once, for just as she stepped off the bottom stair into the foyer, she heard the baby's gurgling laughter coming from the back of the house. Relieved, she moved through several rooms toward the sound. Whoever he was with, Mike was obviously content.

The baby's laughter was coming from the kitchen, which Carrie entered through swinging half-doors opening onto a back hall. Mike sat in a high chair that was pulled up next to a round maple table. A tea towel that had been tied around his neck to serve as a bib was speckled with the remains of what had obviously been his dinner. At the moment he was banging a plastic cup against the tray of the high chair and laughing at the white-haired man who sat at the table and made comical faces at him.

As Carrie entered, an older woman with iron-gray hair pulled tight in a bun and a girl of about eighteen with sandy hair and freckles, both of whom were sitting opposite the man at the table, turned toward her with surprised looks.

The man and the older woman got to their feet hastily. "Mrs. Revell . . ." said the woman, smiling a little uncertainly. "Were you worried about the baby?"

"No, not worried really," Carrie replied. "I just wanted to know what had become of him." She moved to the high chair and, looking down at Mike's milk mustache, laughed. "He couldn't be better, I see." She turned to the three people at the table. "You must be Betty and Adam Carney. Josh mentioned you both to me earlier."

"Yes, ma'am." Betty Carney, a short, plump woman in her early sixties, continued to do the talking for the trio. "This is my niece, Gracie Helmstrom. Gracie comes in from town five days a week and helps out."

Gracie's freckled face crinkled in a shy smile as she murmured, "How do you do, Mrs. Revell." The girl's hazel eyes hadn't left Carrie's face from the moment she had stepped into the kitchen. She was clearly intensely interested in the woman whom Joshua Revell had married.

"Please," Carrie said, "sit down, all of you. I didn't mean to interrupt your dinner."

Adam, a tall, raw-boned man, seemed glad to regain his chair. He turned back to Mike and began pretending to try to take the cup from the baby's chubby hand. Mike was delighted with the game.

"We've just finished our dinner," Betty told Carrie. "So has Mike." Instead of sitting down, she moved to the sink and wet a washcloth, bringing it to the high chair to clean the baby's face and hands. "I heard him when I passed by your bedroom a little while ago. I knocked, but you were sleeping. So I peeked in to make sure the baby was all right. You looked to be resting so well that I decided to bring him down here and see if he was hungry." She carried the wet cloth back to the sink, then turned to look at Carrie a little anxiously. "I hope you don't think I was presumptuous."

"Of course not," Carrie assured her. "I appreciate your feeding Mike. He seems to be enjoying himself immensely."

Betty Carney's smile, resting on the baby, was indulgent. Mike had evidently made a conquest of the Carneys. "He has a good, hearty appetite, all right. I didn't see a bottle anywhere in your bedroom, so I took a chance and gave him a cup. He does right well with it."

Carrie chuckled. "*Now* he does. You should have seen him two months ago when I started giving him liquids from a cup. I just let him spill and slop until he taught himself to handle it. I—I hadn't had any experience with babies before Mike, so I didn't know how else to go about it."

"That's as good a way as any," the housekeeper said, her gaze containing an element of curiosity. "The baby's your nephew, Mr. Josh said." There was a question in the intonation.

"Yes. My sister died when he was born."

After a brief silence, the housekeeper evidently realized her new mistress was not willing to volunteer any more information. She looked somewhat flustered and said, "Would you like your dinner now, Mrs. Revell?"

"No," Carrie said quickly. "We had sandwiches earlier. But I would like a cup of coffee if there's any left in that pot on the stove."

The housekeeper took a cup and saucer from the cabinet, saying, "Wouldn't you like me to bring it to you in the front sitting room? There's a nice fire going in there. I'll bring the baby in, too, if you want."

"That won't be necessary," Carrie said. "I'll drink it here." She had already seated herself in one of the chairs at the table before she realized that the three servants were looking decidedly uncomfortable. "I'm sorry," she said falteringly. "Am I intruding on a family conversation?"

"Not at all!" Adam Carney turned from playing with the baby, and his deep, booming voice was something of a surprise to Carrie.

"It's just that," his wife said as she set Carrie's coffee in front of her, "we aren't used to—" She halted abruptly, her round face flushing, and turned to begin placing the dirty dishes in the dishwasher.

"She means," piped Gracie suddenly, "the other one never set foot in the kitchen."

Adam Carney set his coffee cup down in his saucer

with a loud clatter and scowled at the girl. His wife straightened from her work and said sharply, "Gracie! That will do."

"But," the wide-eyed Gracie prattled on, as if once loosed her tongue could not be reined so quickly, "you told me yourself that Helen Revell was awful keen on servants keeping their place."

Adam's chair scraped against the tile floor as he got to his feet. "Time you was going home, girl. Come along and I'll drive you."

Apparently realizing that she had said something amiss, the girl blushed furiously and followed her uncle from the kitchen without another word.

"You mustn't mind Gracie," the housekeeper said, returning to stacking dishes. "She's a good girl, but when she opens her mouth there's no telling what might come out."

"Helen Revell. That was Josh's first wife, wasn't it?"

The housekeeper's expression was a mixture of curiosity and discomfort. "Why, yes, ma'am. But then I'm sure Mr. Revell has told you that."

"No—uh, we never really discussed his first wife. Did she—well, did she look anything like me?"

Now Betty Carney's mouth fell open. "Like you? Gracious no! She was blond—blonder than Mr. Josh— and very tall, like a model. Not exactly beautiful, you know, but she caught people's eyes, especially—well, I'm sure you don't want to hear about that."

Carrie, whose curiosity was aroused, found that she did want very much to hear more about the first Mrs. Joshua Revell. But she didn't know how to question Betty further without embarrassing her. Nevertheless, she was about to pursue the subject, in spite of what the housekeeper might think, when a harsh buzzing sounded in the kitchen.

"That's Mrs. Revell," Betty said. "If you will excuse me, ma'am, I'll go and see what she wants."

Carrie turned her attention to Mike and was playing pattycake with him when the housekeeper returned to the kitchen. "I'm going to take Mrs. Revell some hot tea." She stopped and smiled at Mike, who was clapping his hands happily. "What a precious child he is. Mrs. Revell asked if you and the baby could come in to see her for a bit. She—she gets lonely, I'm afraid."

"Of course we'll go in," Carrie said willingly. "Won't we, Mike?" She removed the tea towel from his neck, laid it aside, and lifted the baby from the high chair. "Thank you for the coffee, Mrs. Carney, and for feeding Mike."

"Call me Betty like everybody else does. As for feeding that little imp, it was a pleasure. Whenever you need someone to keep an eye on him, just call on me."

"Why, thank you, Betty," Carrie said warmly. "That's very nice of you."

As she turned to carry Mike from the kitchen the housekeeper said, "I'm glad you've come here, ma'am. Mr. Josh, he's needed a wife for a long time now."

Carrie managed a smile but did not reply as she left the kitchen. The good-hearted Betty Carney would never be able to understand the true state of affairs between her and Josh. No more than Ethel Revell would. Better to leave both women in ignorance, Carrie told herself, as she carried Mike along the carpeted hallway toward Ethel's apartment—although how long the two women could go on believing that her marriage to Josh was a normal, happy one, while living under the same roof with them, was subject to conjecture. She wondered, for instance, what Ethel thought of her son's leaving his wife on their wedding day to go to his office. Carrie hoped, as she stood outside the closed door to her mother-in-law's apartment, that Ethel did not bring up that subject with her. In spite of her distrust of all Revells, she had warmed to the woman during their first meeting. She hoped they could be friends, but that might be difficult if Carrie had to be constantly on guard against probing questions. With the servants, she could simply refuse to answer. That might be more difficult where Josh's mother was concerned.

Shifting Mike in her arms, she knocked, heard Ethel's welcome call, and entered the apartment. She found herself in another small sitting room, this one furnished in a more elegant style than the one where she had met Ethel earlier. A gracefully carved antique settee and chairs upholstered in lavender velvet were arranged on one side of the room, and a Persian rug covered most of the floor.

Ethel Revell, in a soft pink velvet robe, was half reclining on a damask rose chaise longue near a corner bookshelf with an exquisite antique desk. She smiled as Carrie and Mike appeared and patted an armchair next to the longue. "Thank you for coming in to see me. Sit down here."

Carrie settled Mike on her lap where, for the moment, he seemed content to gaze with wide blue eyes about the unfamiliar room.

"Oh, here's Betty with my tea."

The housekeeper carried a tray into the room and set it on a low table next to the chaise. "Good," continued Ethel as Betty left, "she's brought two cups. Would you like tea, Carrie?"

"No, thank you. I just had a cup of coffee in the kitchen."

Ethel poured her own tea, added a lump of sugar, and settled back against the chaise longue with the cup in her slender, blue-veined hands. "I'm sorry Josh felt he had to take care of business today." A small frown etched lines between her brows. "I hope you aren't feeling neglected, my dear. Really, I felt it was quite unnecessary for him to go down to the office, and I told him so." She sighed. "As I am sure you have discovered, my son isn't easily swayed in any of his decisions."

"I've noticed," Carrie replied with a wry smile. "But I'm not feeling neglected. I knew when I married Josh that he runs a large corporation which takes a great deal of his time."

"It's unusual to find such understanding in one so young." Ethel sipped her tea, then returned the cup to the tray beside her. Mike was fidgeting in Carrie's lap now, and the older woman brought a small rubber duck from the folds of her robe. "Look what I have for you, Mike." The baby took the toy and began chewing on it contentedly, causing both women to laugh. "That should keep him occupied for a few minutes. I intend to keep several toys for him here so that he will enjoy coming to visit me. Ah . . ." She looked at Carrie with a soft expression. "There is nothing quite like having a baby in the house. But they grow up so quickly."

"That's what everyone tells me," Carrie agreed, "and looking back on it, the past ten months seem to have flown. I must admit that, at the time, I thought those first few weeks would never pass."

"Oh, yes," Ethel commiserated, "that short period of time when they demand such constant attention can be hectic. But it's all worth it. Even when you lose them later. I—I'm sure that Josh must have told you that my younger son, Danny, was killed over a year ago."

"Yes."

"I still miss him dreadfully," Ethel went on. "He was always so full of life. Oh, he was a handful, growing up, but I honestly believe that having Danny to cope with is what saved my sanity when my husband died. Josh, of course, was so involved in the business that I hardly saw him."

Carrie was beginning to feel decidedly uncomfortable at the direction the conversation was taking. "Josh has told me only a little about the scope of the Revell businesses," she said, seeking to steer the talk into other channels. "There is a paper mill and a plywood plant in town, I believe, in addition to the lumbering operation? I don't know whether Josh told you, but I worked for one of your retail lumber outlets when I first moved to Boise."

"Yes, he did," Ethel said. "I believe he said that's how you met."

Carrie murmured her assent, unsure exactly what Josh had told his mother about their relationship in Boise and not wanting to say the wrong thing. Really, he should have briefed her more thoroughly!

"Did you perhaps meet Danny, too?"

"I—I believe I saw him once, but I never got to know him." Carrie really had no choice but to conceal the truth, but she didn't like doing it.

To her relief, Ethel seemed willing to let the subject of Danny drop now. "Carrie, I want you to know how happy I was when Josh called to say he was getting married again. He's been so alone since Helen died so tragically in that hotel fire."

"Hotel fire?" The words were out before Carrie had time to realize that they might sound too morbidly curious.

"Yes, didn't Josh tell you? Helen had gone to Toronto for a few days. The hotel where she was staying burned down. I—I expect Josh didn't tell you because it's still painful for him to talk about. He never speaks of Helen to me, either. My elder son has always kept his own counsel. As his wife, you will be able to get him to talk about his feelings more than I can."

"Ummm," Carrie murmured while thinking that her husband was even less likely to confide in her than in his mother. It was becoming evident that Ethel was expecting a great deal from this marriage, and Carrie felt sad that the older woman, whom she was coming to like, must ultimately be disappointed. But she had hardly had time to digest the new information about Josh's first wife and to wonder fleetingly what Helen had been doing in Toronto without Josh when Betty Carney knocked and opened the door to say, "Mrs. Thorpe is here to see you, Mrs. Revell."

"Jessie?" Ethel said eagerly. "Tell her to come in, Betty." Turning to Carrie, she added, "Jessica Thorpe is a dear family friend. Her father and my husband grew up together."

The woman who stepped into the room, trailing the aroma of an expensive French perfume, was striking—tall, with black hair and the excellent facial bones that make for classic beauty. Her hair was pulled back into a loose chignon, exposing to good effect high cheekbones, a straight patrician nose, and large brown eyes. She was built and moved like a model, Carrie noticed, and the thought caused her to recall that the housekeeper had used the same description in speaking of Josh's first wife. Helen had been blond, however, while this woman's beauty was of the dark exotic variety. She couldn't help reflecting that Josh seemed to be surrounded by beautiful women, she felt self-consciously inadequate by comparison.

Jessica Thorpe crossed the room and bent to kiss Ethel's cheek. "You're looking well, darling."

"I'm feeling well, thank you, Jessie," Ethel said, taking the woman's hand in her own for a brief moment. "It's so good of you to call. I want you to meet Josh's new wife and son, Carrie and Mike."

Jessica straightened to gaze down at Carrie with undisguised curiosity. "Hello, Carrie. I wanted to be one of the first to welcome you to town."

"Thank you," Carrie replied and shifted the baby, who was becoming restless again.

The black-haired woman's large, expressive eyes moved to Mike and she exclaimed, "What a precious child!" But there was a note of falseness in the statement and her laugh sounded brittle to Carrie. "Although I must say I can't imagine Josh in the role of a parent."

"You're in for a surprise, then," Ethel told her amiably. "Josh is quite taken with this young man. In fact, I fear Carrie is going to have to be on guard lest Josh spoil him."

"Incredible!" exclaimed Jessica as she threw off a mink-trimmed black coat, exposing a clinging emerald-green dress that molded itself to her fine figure. She sat down at the foot of the chaise longue beside Ethel. "Where is the new father?"

Ethel glanced at Carrie, waiting for her to reply. "Josh went down to the office to go through his mail," Carrie said.

Jessica's dark brows rose. "Really? What an unromantic bridegroom."

Something in the black-haired woman's manner irritated Carrie and, somewhat to her own amazement, she heard herself saying, "Not all the time." What a liar you are, Carrie told herself. But then, remembering the way Josh had kissed her earlier that afternoon, she realized that her words were not entirely false and felt her cheeks grow warm with the memory.

"But of course," Jessica was saying and a complacent smile settled on her mouth, as if she had had occasion to know this from personal experience. Her dark eyes narrowed as they ran over Carrie's jeans and the chambray shirt, rumpled by Mike's fidgeting, and Carrie wished that she had been dressed a little less casually for this encounter. She was glad when Jessica turned her attention back to Ethel. "It's going to be nice for you, having another woman in the house. I know that Josh can't give you much time. One must pay the price for having a successful son."

"How right you are," Ethel agreed. "But I am

hoping that Josh will be spending more time at home now that Carrie and Mike are here."

"Knowing Josh," said Jessica dryly, "I wouldn't count too much on that."

Why the woman's every statement should rankle so Carrie could not say, but she had to bite her tongue to keep from sounding downright snide. She managed to content herself with a murmured "Perhaps Mike and I will have to spend some time with him at work, then."

"Why, yes," Ethel said, "he will want to show you through the plants. I'm sure he will appreciate your showing an interest in the business, Carrie. I'm afraid Helen never did."

"I don't think Josh has time for conducting guided tours," Jessica put in succinctly.

"I hope," said Carrie, restraining herself from gritting her teeth, "he won't put his wife and son in quite the same category as ordinary tourists."

Jessica's eyes regarded her steadily for a moment, and then she turned to Ethel to say brightly, "I see the rosewood clock has arrived." She indicated a beautiful timepiece displayed in the corner bookshelf.

"It came several days ago," Ethel told her. "Doesn't it go well with the furnishings in this room? I can't thank you enough for finding it for me. I'm just not up to ferreting through antique shops these days, much to my chagrin."

"The moment I saw it," Jessica said, "I knew it was perfect for you."

"As usual," responded Ethel, "your taste is exquisite."

"Do you like antiques?" Jessica inquired of Carrie.

"Yes—I mean, I don't know much about them, but I think Ethel's pieces are quite beautiful."

"Jessie is much more of a connoisseur than I am," Ethel said. "You must see her collection."

"I'd be delighted to have you come by whenever it's

convenient," Jessica said without a pause, yet Carrie couldn't help wondering how sincere the invitation really was.

"Mike keeps me very busy," Carrie said, "but thank you. Perhaps in a few weeks we can get together." Carrie told herself hopefully that in a few weeks Jessica would have forgotten all about the invitation, for she had no desire to meet this self-assured female on her own ground.

"Tell me, Jessie," Ethel said, "how are plans for the holiday bazaar progressing?" With a glance toward Carrie, she added, "We've had a bazaar at Thanksgiving time for the last ten or eleven years. The proceeds go to our local hospital."

Ethel and Jessica plunged into a discussion of the booths planned by the bazaar committee, of which Jessica was chairperson. Carrie listened quietly while trying to keep Mike contented. He was growing bored with being held and seemed determined to get down on the floor. Finally Carrie put him down, but she kept him close to her by hanging on to a romper strap.

It was obvious, from the conversation between the other two women, that they knew one another well and were quite fond of each other. Jessica Thorpe was clearly a frequent visitor, and Carrie found that this knowledge did not sit very well with her. She hoped she would be able to avoid most of Jessica's visits by pleading Mike's need for her attention.

Finally Jessica took her leave, calling breezily over her shoulder that Carrie must call whenever she had a free afternoon. When she was gone, Ethel remarked, "Jessie's always so considerate. With all her civic activities, she manages to find the time to call on me once a week or so." She paused to look at Carrie reflectively for a moment. "Perhaps I should tell you, before you hear it from someone else. Everyone expected Josh and Jessie to marry."

"I'm surprised that such a beautiful woman isn't already married," Carrie said in a carefully noncommittal tone.

"Oh, she was. Her husband died several years ago. He left her well provided for, so she's never had to seek employment. She manages to fill her time with worthwhile projects such as the holiday bazaar, which is very commendable."

"Of course," Carrie murmured. "Ethel—"

"Now, I thought you were going to call me Mother."

"I'm sorry. I'll get used to it in a few days. Mother, I think I'd better see to Mike's bath and put him down for the night."

"The poor little dear has had a full day," Ethel agreed. "Look how he's rubbing his eyes."

Carrie picked up the baby. "I've enjoyed our visit."

"I want you to come often," Ethel told her. "You're welcome any time." She smiled warmly. "I think you're going to be very good for my son."

Going up the stairs, Carrie decided that Ethel Revell was a woman who believed what she wanted to believe. Things were either black or white to her. Josh had married Carrie; therefore, in Ethel's mind, he loved her. Any other reason for her son's marriage would be totally unacceptable in Ethel's comfortable little world. And even though she probably would have preferred Jessica Thorpe as a daughter-in-law, she was prepared to approve of Josh's choice.

Upstairs, Carrie ran warm water into her luxurious bathtub and undressed Mike. She set him down and watched him play with the rubber duck, which he had carried up with him from Ethel's apartment. After a while, she bathed and dried him and dressed him in warm flannel pajamas.

But even as she was thus occupied, her mind kept returning to the meeting with Jessica Thorpe. Everyone had thought Josh and Jessica would marry, Ethel had said. Something told Carrie that Jessica Thorpe had believed that, too. She had come today to get a good look at the woman who had snatched Josh from under her nose—legally, at any rate.

Carrie wondered suddenly if Josh was in love with the beautiful Jessica. If so, this "marriage of convenience" could certainly prove to be inconvenient for the two of them. Carrie found that it was quite easy to imagine them together. She also found that she did not particularly like the intimate scenes between Josh and Jessica that her imagination was conjuring up, and she pushed the images aside with determination.

Her fears that Josh might have married her partly because she reminded him of his first wife seemed unfounded. Apparently he wanted nothing but Mike from the relationship, and if he chose to satisfy his other needs with Jessica, that was their business. Surely they would be discreet enough to keep such a relationship hidden.

In which case, Carrie told herself firmly, she needn't even think about it.

Chapter Four

It was some time before Mike was willing to go unprotesting to his bed. Even though he was tired, he was still keyed up by the day's activities. Carrie finally resorted to rocking the crib gently until he fell asleep.

Then she slipped quietly from the small room, pulling the doors closed behind her, and went back to the bathroom to luxuriate in a long bubble bath.

After drying herself, she wrapped a towel around her body and went to the dresser drawer where she had placed her nightgowns. On top of the stack was the scanty white shorty that had been Jan's wedding present to her. As Carrie's fingers touched the gauzy material she remembered opening the gift in the Boise apartment before Josh came to take her to the judge's chambers.

"Jan, you shouldn't have," Carrie had protested, knowing that her friend had paid more than she could afford for the gift.

"Every bride needs at least one sexy nightgown," Jan had replied.

Carrie had started to say something about the gown being wasted on her, since she would be spending her wedding night alone, but then decided to let the matter drop. Ever since Jan had heard of her plans to marry Josh, she had insisted on taking a romantic view of the situation. Carrie saw no reason to throw cold water on her friend's impulsive generosity.

Now she lifted the gown from the drawer and looked at it with a wry smile. With careless movements she disengaged the towel, letting it fall to the floor, and slipped the gown over her head. Then, standing in front of a full-length mirror that rested on a stand in one corner of the room, she surveyed her reflection. Narrow straps held up a lace bodice that plunged to the high waistline between her breasts, the transparent skirt falling from just below her breasts to midthigh. She might as well have been naked, Carrie mused, noting that the gown's sheerness hid very little.

However, since no one but herself was going to see it, she decided to leave it on so that she could tell Jan truthfully, if she ever asked, that she had worn it on her wedding night. Turning off all the lights except the bedside lamp, she crawled into bed, pulling the covers up around her, and began to leaf through a magazine she'd bought earlier to read on the plane.

She had read two articles and a short story when she heard sounds coming from Josh's suite. She reached out to switch off the lamp, wanting to feign sleep in case Josh should come into the room. After several minutes she heard nothing more and decided that her husband had gone to bed. She didn't feel sleepy, so she turned the lamp back on and searched through the magazine for something else to read.

She was five paragraphs into another story when

suddenly the door to Josh's suite opened and he stood there, a wineglass in each hand, wearing a toast-colored velour robe tied with a wide belt at the waist and reaching to his knees. Below the robe, his long, muscular legs were bare, and Carrie had the abrupt instinctive knowledge that beneath the robe he was naked.

The magazine slid from her hands, and she reached for the sheet that had slipped down to her waist, pulling it up to her chin. "What do you want?"

He came slowly toward the bed, and Carrie saw strange fires burning in the golden depths of his eyes. "What a provocative question. Do you really need to ask what I want?" He sat on the side of the bed, his glance raking over the smoothness of her hair and resting on her lips which were slightly parted in surprise.

"I was almost asleep," she began, gripping the sheet about her shoulders even tighter.

"Don't lie to me. I saw the light under your door and the magazine you were reading when I came in."

Her stomach muscles tensed as she looked into his dark, handsome face, wishing she knew how to force him to stop coming and going here as if they were married in more than name only.

He held her gaze for a moment, then said, "I want my wife to have a glass of wine with me before retiring."

"I don't want any wine," she said, watching him carefully, wondering if he would leave if she threatened to call for help. Not likely, since he knew she wouldn't want to wake Mike.

Then, as if he saw in her face some of the confusion she was feeling, he said quietly, "Please, Carrie. It seems little enough to ask."

"Little enough? You have already taken my freedom and Mike, and now you want—" She bit her lip, for to finish what she had been thinking would probably only encourage him.

"Stop behaving like a convent-educated adolescent." He frowned and pushed one of the wineglasses toward her. "Drink this before you make me so angry I force it down you."

Seeing in his eyes that he was deadly serious, Carrie slowly tucked the sheet across her body just below her armpits and took the glass from his outstretched hand. Sipping sparingly, she watched him over the rim.

He seemed to relax and drank from his own glass. "This is one of the best French wines made. Do you like it?"

"I—it's all right," she murmured. "I know little about wines."

"Among other things?" There was a devilish glint in his eyes now. "You know little about men, too. Am I right?"

"Whether I do or not," Carrie flared, "I do not intend discussing it with you."

"Ah . . ." He sipped his wine. "Well, you needn't tell me, but you don't have to." His glance slid to the narrow straps of her gown. "You chose white for your wedding night, and I think quite appropriately. But what I saw of the gown wasn't what you would call modest. Seduction and innocence—a charming combination."

"You—you're disgusting!" She looked at him with scorn twisting her soft lips. "For your information, this gown was a gift from Jan."

He shrugged. "Still, you chose to wear it tonight."

"It was on top of the stack. I didn't expect anyone else to see it." She set her wineglass on the bedside table. "Please leave. I told you earlier that I can never accept you as my husband."

"Be realistic, Carrie." He frowned and, finishing his wine, set the glass beside hers. "You can't expect me to behave like a brother when I have given you my name. It's true I couldn't allow Mike to be cheated of his heritage, but I didn't have to marry you. I could have gotten Mike by other means. But I knew that you loved him, and I'm not such a monster that I wanted to separate the two of you."

"Well, you have us both now," Carrie said, "but still you want more."

He shrugged. "I'm human enough to want the woman who bears my name. If you would forget the past and let yourself go, I think you would find that you receive as much as you give. Love is good for a woman, Carrie. It gives her a special kind of beauty."

"Love!" Carrie looked at him in total incredulity. "You're unbelievable!"

"I'm a man," he said quietly.

Carrie bit her lip and turned her head away from him. "And you," he went on lazily, "are a woman, a lovely woman."

"Not the sort of woman you seem to think," she said in low tones.

"Aren't you, my dear?" He gave a quiet laugh and, bending his head, placed his warm lips on the smooth curve of her cheek. "How inexperienced you are, but it will be a pleasure to instruct you." His hand pulled the sheet down and pressed warmly against the curve of one breast.

Carrie tried to pull away from him. "I—I'm cold." She tugged at the sheet, but his hand refused to be dislodged and now his fingers, shockingly familiar, were searching the ripe outlines. Carrie's face flushed and, with resentful nervousness, she squirmed back against the pillows in an effort to escape the tormentingly sensual movement of his hand.

He lifted his head and looked down into her wide eyes, holding her gaze as if he intended to hypnotize her. Then his big hand pulled the sheet down to her

waist with one swift, sure movement and her upper
body, with its scanty covering of lace, was vulnerably
exposed to his smoldering eyes. She noticed for the first
time that his hair looked damp, as if he'd just come
from the shower, and the musky smell of his aftershave
seemed suddenly seductively overpowering.

She gave a tormented little shiver as he slowly
slipped one tiny strap off her shoulder. She lay there,
feeling the heavy beat of her heart, as his eyes
deliberately took in every feminine curve of her body.
His hands were hot on the smooth skin of her upper
arms.

"I am your husband," he said softly. "I have the
right to look at you—all of you."

"I—I want to cover up." She tried to pull away from
him, but she found that she could not free herself from
his insistent strength. She could only gasp helplessly
when he lowered his face to her neck and buried his lips
in the soft skin.

"Have you any idea," he murmured thickly, "how
beautiful and desirable you are? I want you, my wife."

"No!" She struggled in his arms.

"Yes," he whispered, and his lips moved up the line
of her jaw and settled gently on her mouth. She could
taste the wine he had drunk, and as he continued to kiss
her lingeringly she felt as if the potent liquid had
entered her bloodstream, sending a warm electric
shock along all her veins. Something dark and primitive
stirred deep down inside her, and she was aware
dazedly that her hands had somehow found their way to
the back of his neck and were buried in his thick, tawny
hair. Never in her life had she experienced such a
helpless panic of all her senses, alone and without
defense against this man who did not live by any of the
rules she had thought civilized people obeyed. She
became aware slowly that the seductive aroma of his
aftershave was mingled with another, sweeter fra-

grance. Where, she wondered dizzily, had she smelled that before?

The kiss deepened, became probing, demanding, as his tongue invaded the hot moistness of her mouth. Feeling herself being taken over by the strange, lulling power emanating from him, Carrie tried once more to pull away. He allowed her to loosen his hold slightly but, keeping his lips near her own, murmured, "Your mouth is soft and delicious. You shouldn't make it say cold, mean things. It wasn't made for that, it was made for kissing." His tongue traced the outline of her lips slowly, sensuously, and she trembled, causing him to smile lazily. "You see? You like that, don't you? You don't want me to stop. Your body is trembling with desire."

"I—I'm trembling because I'm afraid."

"Oh, no," he drawled, and his head came down so that his lips could push against the lace of her gown and move lightly over the soft curve of her breast. The shock of his kisses made her gasp, and he laughed softly. "Relax, Carrie, and stop fighting me. I'm your husband, and you can't deny me indefinitely. Sooner or later, I will have you."

The sweet aroma seemed stronger now as her face brushed the thick, tawny hair, and suddenly she knew why it seemed familiar. It was the fragrance of the perfume Jessica Thorpe had worn earlier that day. Oh, no, she cried inwardly. He had come to her from that woman, and she was so weak that she was letting him . . .

With all of her strength, she struggled free of his grasp. "If you have me, Josh, it will be by force." She lay pressing back against the pillows as far from him as she could get, panting with fear and self-loathing. The fingers that had been caressing so gently now gripped her arms like a steel vise. "You think so, Carrie? Face it, I almost had you just now. You were feeling a woman's passion."

She lay passively and stared up at him. "I felt nothing—nothing but revulsion! Do you really want a woman who feels that way about you?"

"You little fool!"

"If I'd known before I married you what I would have to endure," she went on relentlessly, "I'd never have come here. I'd have taken Mike to the ends of the earth before I'd have married you."

"It seems I've saddled myself with a frigid little prig!" he sneered insolently.

"I hate you!" Carrie turned her head back and forth on the pillow, tormented by her helplessness in his grasp. "I'll hate you until the day I die."

"Go to the devil!" Josh spoke through gritted teeth. "Suddenly I find you about as desirable as a bedpost." His cruel gaze glinted over her. "What a waste of a lovely gown!" He swung himself off the bed and jerked at the belt of his robe as he turned away from her. "Have your virginal bed to yourself—and welcome to it." He walked toward his suite and disappeared, the door closing with a click behind him.

Carrie lay exactly as he had left her for some time, finally coming to her senses enough to pull the sheet and coverlet up over her trembling body. Never had she glimpsed such bitterness in anyone's face, heard such scorn in anyone's voice. The encounter with her husband left her shaken, nausea curling into a cold ball in her stomach.

Groaning, she drew up her legs, hugging them with her arms in a defensive gesture. It was all too clear to her that she had made a dreadful mistake in coming here. She didn't want to be pulled down to Josh's level, a place where love was nothing more than degrading passion. She would not let him make her into the kind of woman he seemed to want. She would fight him every step of the way.

She slept finally, but it was a fitful slumber filled with fragments of frightening dreams. She felt little rested when she finally awoke to pale sunlight filtering in through the sheer curtains. Mike began to stir, too, and putting on her robe she went into the dressing room to get him. She dressed him in a long-sleeved knit shirt and bibbed overalls, and let him crawl about on the carpet while she put on rust corduroy slacks and a matching V-necked sweater.

Mike had pulled himself up to the foot of the bed and was toddling along, one hand gripping the solid wood. Watching him, Carrie realized that it was only a matter of a few weeks until he would be walking without assistance.

She heard no sound from Josh's suite but, since it was after eight, she assumed he had already left for the office. This thought gave her a feeling of relief; she would not have to face him again until evening.

Carrying Mike into the kitchen, she found Betty Carney bending over a pastry board, rolling out piecrust. She brushed the flour from her hands and smiled. "I was wondering when the two of you would show up for breakfast. I've got biscuits and bacon all ready, and I'll have some eggs scrambled in a minute."

Carrie settled Mike in the high chair and went to the stove to pour herself a cup of coffee, which she took back to the table. "Has everybody else eaten?"

"Oh, yes," Betty told her cheerfully. "Mr. Josh always eats at seven on weekdays, and I took Mrs. Revell's breakfast in to her a half hour ago." Having broken eggs into a bowl, she mixed them with a wire whip and carried them to the stove to pour the mixture into a frying pan. Stirring slowly, she turned to Carrie. "Mr. Josh always eats breakfast in the dining room.

I've been wondering if you and Mike would like to have breakfast and lunch in there . . . or I could bring it up to your bedroom, same as I do for Mrs. Revell."

"I don't want to make any extra work for you," Carrie said.

The housekeeper's brow creased in a puzzled frown. "That's what I'm here for, ma'am."

"If it's all the same to you," Carrie went on, "Mike and I can have our breakfast here in the kitchen. In fact, I think Mike should have most of his meals here. He's still pretty messy, and I wouldn't want him dropping food on the carpets."

Betty removed the scrambled eggs from the skillet to two plates. "Whatever you want," she said as she carried the plates to the table.

"I'm not used to people waiting on me," Carrie said frankly. "Besides, the idea of eating alone in the dining room doesn't particularly appeal to me."

Betty Carney studied her for a moment, her head to one side. "You're sure not anything like I expected."

Carrie smiled as she handed Mike half of a buttered biscuit. "Oh? What did you expect?"

The housekeeper hesitated. "Someone older and—"

"More sophisticated?" Carrie provided lightly. "Oh, don't be embarrassed, Betty. I can imagine what you expected. But I'm just a small-town girl who lived from one paycheck to the next until now."

"It's no crime to have to work for a living," sniffed Betty.

"No, but you'll have to give me a little time to get used to the way the Revells live."

Betty smiled warmly. "I hope you don't change too much, ma'am, if I may say so."

When she'd finished her breakfast, Carrie said, "May I leave Mike here with you for a while? I'd like to go in to see Mrs. Revell."

"You go along," Betty responded readily. "I'll set his

playpen up in the corner and he can keep me company this morning."

Carrie found Ethel, wearing a white satin robe, sitting at her antique desk writing a letter. Calling for Carrie to enter, Ethel laid her pen aside and moved to sit on the chaise longue. "I'm glad you could come in for a bit."

"I don't mean to interrupt what you're doing."

Ethel indicated the armchair next to the chaise. "Sit down. I can write letters any time. It's a note to Jessica thanking her formally for finding the clock for me." Her pale face sobered. "Josh left very early this morning, didn't he?"

Carrie almost said that she had no idea when Josh had left, but she caught herself just in time. "About seven. I'm not sure of the exact time because Mike didn't awaken me until later."

"Josh works too hard," stated Ethel. "I'm expecting you to use your wifely charms to keep him at home more."

Carrie felt her cheeks growing warm and looked away from her mother-in-law in an effort to hide her discomfort. She could feel Ethel's eyes resting steadily on her face, however, and after a pause the older woman said, "Josh is very like his father was, my dear. Strong and domineering, if you allow him to get away with it. But a shrewd woman can get her way with a man who loves her."

Carrie cast about for something to say to this sweet, misguided woman. "His work piled up while he was in Boise," she managed finally, "but I imagine he'll get caught up in a few days."

"I expect you're right," Ethel said. "There's still coffee in the pot Betty brought in earlier. Would you like a cup?"

"Yes, thank you," said Carrie gratefully, willing to

agree to anything that would switch the topic of conversation from her husband.

Ethel lifted the silver pot which sat on the small table beside her and poured coffee into a fragile china cup, which she then handed to Carrie. "I've been wanting to discuss something with you—a small dinner party I'm planning for Saturday evening to introduce you to our closest friends."

"Are you sure you're feeling up to a party?" Carrie inquired, feeling the beginning of dread at the prospect of being on show all Saturday evening as the lovely wife.

Ethel laughed. "I'm certainly up to planning the menu, which is all that is required of me until the guests arrive. Betty will take care of everything else. I thought we might serve Cornish hens. Betty glazes them with an orange confection and serves them with a delicious wild-rice dressing. Or perhaps you would prefer something else?"

"No, that sounds fine."

"Good, then I'll call everyone today. We'll have Loren and Christine McCloy. Loren is manager of our paper mill. Christine's always busy with their three youngsters, but I think you'll like her. I want you to get acquainted with some of the women in town who are nearer your own age. Of course, Kevin Hamilton, the manager of our plywood plant, must be included."

"And Mrs. Hamilton?" Carrie put in.

"Kevin's a bachelor." Ethel chuckled. "But two or three unattached young women are working on changing that status. Oh, we must have our local physician, Robert Marlow, and his wife, Jane. The Marlows have been good friends ever since Robert came here to practice more than twenty years ago. Let's see, now . . ." She gazed across the sitting room reflectively. "Oh, we can't forget Jessica." Her eyes came back to Carrie with innocent sincerity. "That will round out the number nicely, don't you think?"

Carrie murmured in agreement, although at the mention of Jessica Thorpe a small feeling of anticipation, which might have been stirring in her as Ethel enumerated the Revells' closest friends, was quickly doused. Her first impression had been the correct one: Saturday night was going to be an ordeal.

That afternoon, while Mike napped, Carrie explored the house and grounds. The Carneys occupied a small apartment in one of the single-story wings which angled off the main section of the house, while Ethel's suite of rooms took up most of the other wing. The large two-story central section contained, on the ground level, formal living and dining rooms, kitchen and utility areas, a book-lined study, and two small, cozy sitting rooms. Upstairs, in addition to Carrie's and Josh's suites, there were four unoccupied bedrooms, each with its own bath. These, Carrie surmised guiltily, had undoubtedly been planned to accommodate the children Josh would have someday. Now, except for the one that Mike would use later, they would continue to be unoccupied—unless Josh came to his senses and allowed her to get a divorce and leave with Mike so that he could marry again.

The grounds covered, as she had already concluded, several acres; a tall chain-link fence surrounded the entire estate. Most of the acreage had been left to flourish in its wild state, and a variety of trees grew in dense profusion. Scattered about were several stone benches which Carrie realized would be lovely spots for idling away quiet hours during the spring and summer months. Near the house, Adam Carney had taken nature in hand, creating a smooth rolling lawn with well-spaced spruce and pine trees, shrubbery, and flower beds.

She recalled Josh's statement when he had brought her here: *A good place for a child to grow up.* It was true; this was far more suitable than anything Carrie could have provided for Mike. The knowledge made her feel sad as she returned at dusk to the house. There the housekeeper asked if she would like to have her dinner with Mrs. Revell in her suite. Josh, it seemed, had not come home. Betty insisted on feeding Mike in the kitchen, and Carrie accepted Ethel's invitation, not wanting to dine alone.

While she and Ethel were eating at a table set up by Betty in Ethel's sitting room, Josh phoned.

"I'm sorry to miss dinner," he told Carrie, his voice sounding brusque and far away. "We've got a problem with some late lumber deliveries, and I've spent most of the day on the phone soothing disgruntled customers. I only now have a chance to look at the day's mail." He paused to heave a deep sigh. "I'm going to be very late, I'm afraid."

"I see."

"I doubt that you do," he stated flatly. "Mother gave me a rakedown last evening, and I expect I'm in for another one from her after this. Try to explain the situation, will you?"

"I will."

She hung up, feeling irritated that Josh expected her to make his excuses for him. Wasn't he the one who had insisted that they play the part of a happily married couple? For Mike's sake, he had said. He certainly hadn't sounded concerned about Mike just now; he hadn't even asked about him.

She couldn't help thinking that Josh, with all those employees at his beck and call, could have come home for dinner if he had wanted to. Perhaps, she thought bitterly, he plans to dine with Jessica Thorpe. Grimly, she walked back to the table to answer Ethel's questioning look the best way she could.

She played with Mike for some time before putting him to bed, retiring herself a little before eleven. Josh was still not home, and her suspicion that he was with Jessica had hardened into certainty.

Next morning she was awakened by the sounds of deep male laughter and childish gurgling coming from Mike's room. The louvered doors were standing open; evidently Josh had gone in to say good morning before leaving for work. Tying her quilted cotton robe about her waist, Carrie went into the bathroom to wash her face and brush her hair. She lingered for some time, wanting to give Josh ample opportunity to go downstairs for breakfast. But when she reentered the bedroom, he and Mike were sitting on her bed. Josh was still in his robe, and Mike was playing with his Teddy bear.

Carrie stammered, "I—I'd better change Mike's diaper."

"I already did." Josh glanced up at her and laughed shortly. "Don't look so shocked. It's not all that difficult."

She walked across the bedroom to sit in the velvet-padded dressing-table chair. "It's just that I can't picture you doing—that."

His tawny brows rose sardonically. "No? I'm finding that I have a strong inclination toward fatherhood. Speaking of that, I talked to my attorney yesterday about the adoption. He's going to draw up the papers. He'll let us know when we can go down to the judge's office and sign them."

"We? Why do I have to sign anything?"

"He found no record that you had ever legally adopted Mike."

Carrie was astonished. "Why, I didn't. I just assumed it wasn't necessary. Meg asked me to raise him."

He shrugged. "In all likelihood, no problems would

have arisen if I hadn't learned about Mike's parent-
age."

"You needn't remind me of that!"

"Now it seems wise," he went on levelly, as if she
hadn't spoken, "for both of us, as husband and wife, to
go through all the legal formalities of adoption. Then
there won't be any unexpected problems later."

"I see," Carrie responded, pressing her lips together.
She didn't like being reminded that her problems had
increased tremendously after Josh had learned about
Mike. On the other hand, she did want to be Mike's
legal mother, even if she had to accept Josh as his father
into the bargain.

She changed the subject. "Your mother wasn't very
happy with you for being so late last night."

He gave her a glacial look. "I'm sure I'll hear all
about it when I stop by her apartment later. I don't care
to be taken to task by my wife as well."

Carrie stiffened. "Far be it from me to criticize how
you spend your time! I couldn't care less, actually. I do
hope, for your mother's sake, you will be here for the
dinner party she is planning for Saturday evening."

"Oh, no!" He reached out to retrieve Mike's stuffed
bear, absentmindedly handing it back to the baby.
"Must we be subjected to that so soon? Why didn't you
veto the idea?"

"I don't look forward to it any more than you do,"
Carrie said fervently, "but I'd no intention of hurting
your mother's feelings. She wants to introduce me to
your friends. How could I explain that I don't care to
meet your friends—unless I tell her the truth about this
so-called marriage?"

Unwilling to meet his cynical gaze, she turned toward
the dressing-table mirror and, picking up a brush,
began giving her dark hair a second, unnecessary
brushing. In the mirror, she saw Josh setting Mike
down on the carpet with his bear. He strode across the

room and stood behind her, meeting her look in the mirror.

"You won't tell Mother anything about our relationship."

Carrie laid the hairbrush down slowly. "I'm to play the loving wife Saturday night, is that it?"

"Exactly," he sneered. "It is to be hoped that you can pull it off. The role is so contrary to your true attitude."

"No more than your role as a considerate husband differs from the real Josh Revell," she retorted.

The gold-flecked eyes widened slightly and stared at her in the mirror. Abruptly, his hand came to rest at the back of her neck, entangled in her hair. The heat from his fingers penetrated through the sensitive skin of her nape, and when he began a slow massaging motion, she stiffened, wanting to fling his hand away and run from the room. But that would gain her nothing, and she knew it. Mike would be frightened—and, besides, Josh would come after her and, she greatly feared, do something even worse.

"I'd like you to look your best Saturday evening," he said quietly. "If you want to buy something new to wear, I have accounts at most of the stores in town. It isn't Boise, but there are a couple of good women's shops."

"No, thank you," she said, her breath catching a little as his hand continued the sensuous caressing movements on her nape. "Your friends will have to take me as I am—or leave me."

His honey-tipped lashes moved closer together as his eyes narrowed. "It's likely that the women will dress semiformally."

Carrie bit her lip, stifling a mad impulse to moan and push back against the seductive fingers. "I—I have a long skirt that will go nicely with the blouse I wore with my wedding suit."

"I am sure you will look lovely," he murmured.

For a long moment their mirrored gazes locked, and his fingers stilled. Then, almost as if he had just become aware of what he was doing, he snatched his hand away. "Incidentally, your new car should arrive today. I picked it out yesterday morning."

Yesterday morning? But he had said he was buried in work all day yesterday. How odd that he had taken the time to find a car for her.

"There weren't a great many to choose from in town," he continued, "but I thought you'd prefer having a car right away to waiting months for a special order. If you don't approve of my choice, of course, we will return it."

"No," she stammered. "I'm sure it will be fine."

"Good." He tore his gaze from hers and walked toward his own suite, leaving Carrie feeling strangely as weak as if she'd just finished a stint of strenuous physical exercise.

The car, a red Corvette, arrived just after she had put Mike down for his afternoon nap. Its sleek lines were pleasing to the eye, and Carrie had to admit that she couldn't have chosen anything better suited to her tastes herself. What a maddeningly surprising man Joshua Revell was!

She experienced a feeling of excitement as she looked the car over, and she wanted to take it for a spin immediately. After telling Ethel that she was going to drive into town and getting Betty's promise to look in on Mike, she got into the car. After a few moments spent discovering what all the knobs controlled, she drove slowly down the curving drive and through the estate gates, picking up speed as she approached the small lumber town.

As she descended the slope of the mountain the town was spread out below her, lying along the eastern boundary of the Snake River, the state of Washington on the opposite bank. The area had an interesting history. It was the ancestral home of the Nez Percé Indians and later the location of a large gold strike in the 1860s. In former times, the only visitors to the vast wilderness area had been the legendary mountain men. Probably because the new car was making her feel fanciful, Carrie told herself the mountain men's major characteristics of independence, strength, and a belief in self-rule had been passed down through the families who had lived in the area since that earlier time. This tradition was manifested in men like Joshua Revell.

Mountains rose to the east of the town, with some high prairie areas to the north and south. Carrie drove slowly through the periphery of the residential area until she found the business district. Turning into one of the main streets, she parked near a block of shops and got out, pulling the wool coat up closely under her chin against the brisk wind. As she wandered through several of the shops she couldn't help noticing that workers and shoppers alike eyed her curiously. The town was obviously small enough so that she was identified as a stranger. When the man behind the counter at the drugstore where she had a cup of coffee asked if she was a tourist, she satisfied his curiosity by introducing herself. It was clear, from his reaction, that her husband was greatly admired in the town. That was understandable, since the Revell Corporation was the community's largest employer.

A few minutes later she received a friendly welcome from the owner of a small craft shop, a blond woman in her early thirties named Julia Freemont.

"I've been dying to meet you, Carrie," exclaimed Julia as she pumped Carrie's hand vigorously. "We all have, ever since word got around that Josh was married again. He's well thought of around here, as you've probably already discovered."

Carrie smiled, enjoying the woman's open warmth.

After a few other preliminaries, Julia said baldly, "I want to be the first to capture you for the holiday bazaar. Ethel's probably mentioned it to you."

"As a matter of fact, she has," Carrie admitted.

"I'm in charge of a bakery booth, and I'm still in the process of lining up volunteer help. May I put you down for an afternoon or two? Say, the Friday or Saturday before Thanksgiving? It's expected of a Revell, you know."

Julia Freemont seemed to take it for granted that, as Josh's wife, Carrie would want to help. She found that she couldn't say no to this cheerful, gregarious woman, and before she had left the shop she had promised not only to work in the bakery booth but also to contribute some of her own baked goods for sale.

More than an hour later, as she drove back toward the Revell estate, Carrie reflected with some surprise upon the way she had been accepted by the townspeople she had met. They, like Ethel, seemed to feel a wife was just what Josh had been needing to make his life complete. And, of course, since she was young and attractive, no one doubted that the marriage was a love match.

However, Carrie thought wryly as she turned the car between the stone pillars again, it remained to be seen if that opinion held after the dinner party on Saturday.

Chapter Five

Carrie studied herself in the mirror. She wore a floor-length chocolate velveteen skirt with the new ivory silk blouse. She'd left the first few buttons of the blouse undone to reveal a single strand of tiny pearls, her only piece of real jewelry except for her wedding ring, and she'd pinned an ivory velvet rose trailing long velvet ribbons to the skirt's wide waistband. Her dark brown hair was brushed back from a center part in loose waves, falling to her shoulders in a casual cascade of upcurling strands. She'd applied mascara, eye shadow, blusher, and a wet-look lip gloss, more makeup than she ordinarily used. Despite that, she looked curiously young and vulnerable.

There was a sharp knock. Calling, "Come in," she turned as Gracie Helmstrom thrust her head around the door.

"Mr. Josh wants you to come down now. The guests have arrived."

Carrie smiled at the freckle-faced girl. "Do I look all right?"

Gracie ran her eyes over Carrie and said earnestly, "You look beautiful!"

"Thank you, Gracie." Carrie laughed. "It's nice to know that at least one person in the house approves of my appearance."

"Oh, it isn't only me," said Gracie frankly. "I've seen the way Mr. Josh looks at you, as if he'd like to grab you and kiss you in front of everybody."

Or shake me, thought Carrie, biting her lip. She picked up an atomizer from her dressing table and sprayed a mist of perfume on her wrists. She wondered how much the servants suspected about her true relationship with Josh. They had to know they didn't share the same bed. She had even found herself remarking to Betty once that Mike was often restless at night and she didn't want Josh to be disturbed, and she had hated herself for feeling called upon to offer any sort of explanation.

"Is Mike behaving himself?" she asked the girl.

"He's being a little doll," Gracie assured her. "Aunt Betty's already fed him and put him in his playpen in the kitchen. Uncle Adam's playing with him now." The way the Carneys had taken to the baby, Carrie knew she needn't worry about him.

She turned away from the dressing table and, leaving the bedroom, went slowly along the carpeted hallway and down the wide stairs, lifting her skirt slightly as she descended.

Josh, wearing a dove-gray casual suit with an open-collared black silk shirt, was standing at the foot of the stairs, gazing up into the shadows, a glass in his hand. He stared at her as she reached the foyer.

"Come, I want to introduce you to our guests," he said abruptly, his eyes going over her coolly, and she could not guess what he thought of her appearance.

He took her arm and led her into the formal living room, where all talk ceased at their entrance. Carrie fixed a smile on her face and went forward to meet the Revells' friends.

Loren McCloy was middle-aged, a little above medium height, with light brown hair and eyes. In his well-tailored heather-green suit he looked the part of a successful businessman, and he spoke quietly. His wife, Christine, could not have been more of a contrast to her husband. Short, plump, with tightly curling auburn hair, she spoke quickly, almost breathlessly. Within two minutes of being introduced to her Carrie knew the names and ages of her three children and how they were doing in school.

The more elderly couple, Dr. Robert Marlow and his wife, Jane, could almost have been twins. The doctor was portly and swarthy-skinned and had an impressive head of thick white hair. Jane, his wife, was a large woman with white hair that had been treated with blue rinse the same shade as her floor-length polyester skirt and jacket. She had a remarkably unlined face for a woman in her sixties. Both the Marlows had bright blue eyes and long noses. It soon became clear that Jane was the retiring sort, allowing her husband to do most of the talking for both of them.

The person Carrie had most dreaded seeing, of course, was Jessica Thorpe. Her first sight of Jessica, wearing a tight black crepe gown split to the knee in front and astonishing large diamond earrings in her well-shaped ears, did nothing to bolster Carrie's confidence. Jessica's black hair was pulled back smoothly in an intricate French roll fastened with several small diamond clips. She was standing at one end of the living room, champagne glass in hand, talking to a tall, extremely slender man in his early thirties. The man had dark hair and eyes and well-shaped features that, taken together, still managed somehow to be rather

ordinary looking. He had a warm smile, however, that
made Carrie feel a little more at ease as Josh introduced
the man as Kevin Hamilton.

The introductions made, Josh asked abruptly,
"Would you like a drink?"

"A sherry, please," she said as she turned to answer
Kevin Hamilton's question about her nephew.

Josh fetched her the sherry and she sipped it
gratefully, clasping hands that had suddenly become
damp around the coolness of the crystal glass. She was
conscious of a feeling of disappointment and in that
same instant realized that she had been childishly
hoping Josh would comment favorably on her appearance. Now, standing near the elegantly turned-out
Jessica, she was sure she was dressed too simply.

The living room was a vast expanse of off-white
carpeting and walls broken by several excellent original
oil landscapes. The furnishings were in muted shades of
blue and green, lit by a magnificent crystal chandelier
and several lamps. In the dining room, a large table was
spread with white linen and set with a low centerpiece
of deep rust and amber carnations. China, silver, and
crystal gleamed under the flickering light.

Josh had caught the direction of her look and was
gazing at her with a questioning lift of his brows. "The
table looks lovely," she murmured.

"Mother is a renowned hostess." His smile was
slightly twisted. "You must learn from her, for you will
be taking over those duties soon."

She wanted to reply sarcastically, "My role keeps
expanding." Instead, she heard herself saying in an
uncharacteristically prim voice, "There's so much I
don't know."

"True." The gold-flecked eyes were mockingly
alight, as if it amused him that she was purposely
avoiding controversy with him. "But you are young,
and there is plenty of time."

Noticing that Jessica had drifted across the room to speak with Ethel, she turned away from her husband to the tall, dark-haired man. "Kevin," she said brightly, "I understand you manage the plywood plant. I'm afraid I know very little about the lumber business, but I would like to learn. Perhaps you would show me the plant sometime."

"Certainly." He darted a look at Josh. "But I'm sure Josh would be happy to educate you in the family business."

Josh sipped his drink, his only response a slight tilt of his head. Carrie said, "I don't think my husband has the time or the inclination to play tour guide."

"Kevin doesn't while away his days in idleness either, my dear," said Josh quietly.

"I can always take time for the boss's wife," Kevin responded gallantly.

Josh abruptly detached himself from them and moved to set his empty glass on a convenient side table. Carrie sensed a kind of simmering anger in his withdrawal, but she had no idea what could have inspired it. Perhaps he resented her showing an interest in the family business, more proof that his interest in her, if it existed at all, was purely physical. He merely wanted a warm body on nights when Jessica was otherwise occupied. Once he realized he could not seduce her, she wondered, how long would it be before he decided a divorce was in order? At the moment she was little more than an irritation because she was thwarting his will. But he wasn't a patient man, and she couldn't believe he would accept the status quo indefinitely.

She continued to chat with Kevin and was glad when Ethel announced it was time to go in to dinner. Kevin followed her to the table and took the chair to her right, with the McCloys on her left. Ethel sat at the head of the table, with Josh and Jessica to her right and the Marlows across from the McCloys.

Betty served the first course, vichyssoise, flushing as Josh complimented her on its flavor. She had every right to feel gratified, Carrie thought, as she spooned up some of the thick cold liquid redolent of herbs. It was delicious and she felt it calming her tense nerves.

Across from her, Josh bent his head to hear something Jessica murmured. For no reason, Carrie found herself remembering that recent morning when he had stood behind her at her dressing table, his fingers moving at her nape.

Whenever Josh spoke, the others at the table leaned toward him to listen respectfully, as if they were drawn to the power that emanated from him. Was she any different from the others? Carrie wondered. More than once she had been drawn, too. But the magnetic attraction for her was something instinctive and primitive, something she did not understand and, moreover, feared.

Abstractedly, she heard Ethel's voice asking her kindly if she had finished her vichyssoise and realized, her face flushing, that Betty was standing beside her waiting to take her half-empty soup cup.

Carrie nodded, embarrassed at the way her thoughts had wandered. Ethel turned to Dr. Marlow to say, "Robert, how is your search for an associate progressing?"

"Not very well," said the doctor. "It's difficult to find a young physician these days who wants to go into family practice in a small town."

"It's such a shame," said Jane Marlow in her small, quiet voice that seemed incongruous in such a large woman, "that we had to lose Dr. Wickersham."

This seemingly innocuous remark was met by silence. Looking about the table, Carrie saw that the self-effacing Jane had suddenly commanded everyone's attention. The silence was stifling with tension, and, stirring uneasily, Carrie asked, "What happened to him?"

She was not really interested in what had become of Dr. Marlow's former associate, but she wanted to say something to break the strange mood that had settled at the table. Jane Marlow, however, continued to look down at her plate as she murmured, "He . . . died."

"Oh, that's too bad," Carrie responded, her effort to enliven the conversation faltering.

"Have you placed ads in the medical journals, Robert?" Josh's steady voice seemed to release the others from their spell, as if a collective sigh had gone around the table.

"Oh, yes," replied the doctor with a heartiness that sounded a little forced. "Several times. A few men have contacted me, but, in the end, none of them wanted to come."

"Well, you can't keep carrying the whole load yourself," Ethel said, giving her friend a concerned scrutiny. "Jane tells me that there are nights when you don't sleep more than two or three hours."

"I take catnaps," Robert Marlow responded. "And I'm going to retire in a few years, whether or not I've found anyone to take over my practice. Did Jane tell you we're thinking of looking at condominiums in Florida?"

A lively discussion ensued about the wisdom of retired couples leaving their homes to pass their retirement years in a new environment. The dinner progressed, each course more delicious than the previous one, and Carrie found herself conversing easily with Kevin Hamilton and feeling as if she had known him for years. Wine was served with the meal, and just before they left the table, Dr. Marlow asked for everyone's attention, lifted his glass, and said, "Congratulations to Josh and Carrie, and may they have a long and happy life together."

"Hear, hear!" exclaimed Kevin as glasses were lifted.

Carrie fingered the stem of her own glass, glancing across the table at Josh through lowered lashes. He sipped his wine and gazed at her with a deeply penetrating look. Then, he turned to say something to Jessica, Carrie studied him unobtrusively. His shoulders looked enormously broad in the dove-gray jacket. The strong column of his neck rose from the open collar of the black shirt, his waving tawny hair falling down over the back of the collar slightly. Every last detail about his appearance spoke of money and power.

He glanced up suddenly and caught her eyes staring at him. One tawny eyebrow rose sardonically, and she turned abruptly to Kevin at her side, rushing into a question about the process of making plywood.

They left the table finally, returning to the living room. A few minutes later, seated on a pale blue brocade sofa beside Ethel, Carrie looked about the room and noticed that Josh had disappeared. A further sweeping glance told her that Jessica, too, was gone. The blatantly obvious character of their absence went over Carrie in a humiliating wave. She hardly expected Josh to respect *her,* but how dare he behave with such tactlessness in his mother's presence? To do Ethel credit, she continued to talk amiably with Carrie and Christine. Several minutes later, when Josh and Jessica sauntered back into the room together, Ethel merely glanced up at them and smiled.

Her mother-in-law was the soul of decorum, Carrie realized, and she rather envied the older woman the ability to look so cool in the face of such rude behavior.

A half hour later, although to Carrie it seemed as if days had passed since they left the table, the guests began to make their departures. Finally, when only Carrie, Josh, and Ethel remained, Ethel seemed to sag a little and, smiling at her son and his wife, said that she was tired and wanted to retire.

Getting to her feet, Carrie took the older woman's arm solicitously. "I'm going to bed, too, Mother. I'll walk with you to your apartment."

Josh didn't comment as the two women left the room, and Carrie suspected he was only waiting for them to be out of sight so he could follow Jessica home.

In her bedroom, Carrie looked in on Mike, who was sleeping peacefully in his crib. She closed the louvered doors on him and went into the bathroom to change into a yellow nylon gown. She was standing in front of her dressing table, brushing her hair, when the door from the hallway burst open and Josh strode in.

Laying aside the brush, Carrie turned to face him, feeling exposed in the clinging yellow nylon, even though the gown's Grecian cut was much more modest than the white lace one that she had not worn again since that first night.

"Does it ever occur to you to knock?" she asked querulously.

He smiled coldly. "Not at my wife's door, no."

"Well, I'm too tired to rehash the dinner party," Carrie said, moving to pass him. "I want to go to bed."

"Not quite yet." He had moved between her and the bed, and she halted, her blue-green eyes blazing into his. "I want an explanation of your behavior tonight."

Carrie stood for a moment as if she had been turned to stone. Then she exclaimed, "*My* behavior!"

"What do you think you were doing with Kevin Hamilton?" His words issued from lips which had thinned with anger.

"I was," she retorted with mounting indignation, "being hospitable to a guest in this house."

"You were flirting with him," Josh stated harshly, "and everyone here tonight knew it. You were too obvious to have left any doubt." His icy gaze swept over her, narrowing slightly as it rested on the bodice of her gown where her breasts were clearly outlined against the clinging nylon. "You're a conniving little girl, Carrie," he observed too calmly. "I've suspected all along that there was more beneath that chaste façade of yours than meets the eye."

"What right have you to criticize me?" she demanded shrilly, drawing up her arms in an effort to cover her breasts and hide them from his steady regard. "If you wish to discuss crude flaunting of the proprieties, what were you and Jessica doing when you disappeared after dinner?"

He lifted his head and stared down at her, frowning. "She wanted to ask my advice about an investment she's thinking of making."

"Oh?" Carrie exclaimed, feeling a quaking start deep down inside her. "I had no idea you are an investment counselor, in addition to your other talents!" Her lips twisted with irony. "Good heavens, Josh, what kind of fool do you take me for? *I* don't believe that, and neither will anyone else."

"You're jealous," he drawled, an insightful expression settling on his face.

Carrie felt a shaky little laugh rise in her throat. "No, I'm not!"

"You are," he said in the same sardonic drawl as before. He took a step toward her and her hands came up between them instinctively in an attempt to push him away, but it was useless. His arms came around her with a steely strength, pressing against the small of her back, crushing her body against his.

His mouth covered hers with cruel demand. Her fingers were spread flat against the silk front of his shirt, and she could feel the heat of his skin through the thin material. Carrie felt a sob gathering in her throat. His mouth was crushing hers in an angry sort of persuasion, and the churning that had uncoiled itself somewhere in her midsection was little short of tumultuous. She was shamefully aware that her breasts were straining against his chest in an unwilling yearning.

When at last he lifted his head, she heard herself give a little involuntary groan of protest. He laughed huskily. "You can't have Kevin Hamilton, Carrie. You will have to settle for me."

For a moment Carrie stood still, shocked and motionless, then with a stifled cry she freed one arm in a movement that took him unawares. Before either of them knew what was happening, her open palm had struck his cheek, the impact so great that her whole hand stung.

Josh grabbed her, shaking her. "Carrie you . . ."

"I didn't—mean to do that." She pressed a fist against her trembling lips. "You—you made me so angry—"

Slowly the fury drained from his face and his grip on her loosened. She stepped backward, shaking off his hands. His face darkened again and he took one hesitant step toward her, then halted, obviously puzzled by the bright glitter of tears that had sprung to her eyes.

"Did I hurt you?" he demanded. "Carrie, I—"

"Yes," she interrupted. Her voice was low, but it throbbed with a fierce sincerity that brought his tawny brows together. "You have done nothing but hurt me since the day we met."

His face paled, emphasizing the angry red imprint of her hand on his cheek. Without another word, he moved around her and stormed out through the hallway door. She heard him descend the stairs, then leave the house, with no effort to do it quietly.

During the week that followed, she saw little of him. Two mornings, he came into her bedroom to spend a few minutes with Mike before going to work. But

Carrie might as well have been another piece of furniture, for all the attention he paid her. And she preferred it that way, she told herself.

During the same period that her relationship with her husband had reached an impasse, the one with her mother-in-law grew closer. She spent some time each day with Ethel in her apartment. These hours, and her time with Mike, were, in fact, the only parts of her new life that she really looked forward to.

The two women talked easily about a variety of topics—except when Ethel brought the conversation around to Josh. "You *must* make him spend more time at home," Ethel said on several occasions. Since Carrie did not know now to reply to this, she usually said nothing.

Once Ethel looked at her sharply and asked, "Carrie, has something gone wrong between you and my son?"

"No, everything is just as it was on the day we married," Carrie told her truthfully.

Clearly, Ethel was not satisfied with that. Since she was not a prying mother-in-law, she held her peace, although Carrie found Ethel studying her thoughtfully from time to time.

That week before Thanksgiving, Carrie spent several afternoons with Betty in the kitchen baking fruitcakes and cookies for Julia Freemont's bakery booth. Chatting and working alongside the housekeeper seemed to put Carrie in something of a holiday spirit, and she found that she was looking forward to the bustle of the bazaar.

On Friday morning she took her baked goods to town early and found the large Community Building where the booths had been set up. Julia was manning the bakery booth and she welcomed Carrie's contributions effusively.

"Did you use Betty Carney's recipe for the fruitcakes?"

When Carrie admitted that she had, Julie added, "They'll go like hotcakes. I'm going to put one of them aside for myself while I can."

"When do you want me to take over?" Carrie inquired.

"One o'clock."

"Good. I'll have plenty of time to browse." During the next hour, Carrie bought a stuffed monkey made from men's work socks for Mike, a pretty ceramic pencil holder for Ethel, and some bright potholders for Betty.

The crowd milling in the Community Building increased as the morning passed and by ten-thirty Carrie had seen all of the booths. Since she still had more than two hours to kill before taking her place in Julia's booth, she remembered Kevin Hamilton's offer to show her through the plywood plant. Looking down at the lime-green wool slacks and sweater and champagne-colored wool jacket she had on, she decided that she looked presentable enough to put in an appearance at one of the Revell businesses.

Her decision made, she wove her way through the crowd, hurried to her car, and drove north toward the town's outskirts where the Revell complex spread over several hundred acres.

Kevin Hamilton's office, she was told by a guard at the gate, was in a buff-brick building to the east of the huge metal barnlike structure which housed the plywood plant. She gave her name to Kevin's secretary and had just seated herself in a chair to wait when the door to the inner office opened and Kevin himself grinned at her.

"This is a pleasant surprise, Carrie."

"I won't stay if you're busy."

"I'm not too busy for you. Come on—I'll give you our highest-priced tour."

She laughed and they left the office building, Kevin's

hand resting lightly on her arm. As they walked across the grounds toward the plant she glanced over at him. A rust tan-and-cream-striped sports coat set easily on his long, slender frame. With the coat he wore a tan V-necked sweater and trousers, cream shirt, rust tie, and highly polished cordovan ankle-high walking boots. His clothes, as Carrie had noticed during their previous meeting, were chosen to match perfectly and were clearly expensive.

"I found myself with some time on my hands before my stint at one of the bazaar booths," Carrie explained. "It's kind of you to take time out from what I know is a busy schedule."

His dark eyes rested lightly on her face. "As I said before, I can always take time for the boss's wife. I'm surprised Josh hasn't taken you through the whole complex by now."

"He's busy," Carrie said shortly, "and I'd prefer it if you didn't think of me as the boss's wife."

"A friend, then?"

"That's much better."

"You say that," he commented thoughtfully, "as if you need a friend."

She avoided meeting his glance, afraid he would see too much in her eyes. "We can never have too many."

He said no more until they reached the plant door and he opened it and ushered her through. Taking down two blue cotton hooded coveralls from a rack nearby, he handed one to her, saying, "Put this on and button it all the way up. Otherwise, you'll have sawdust all over you when we come out."

The coverall reached almost to her ankles, and as they entered the noisy, dusty plant she was glad of the protection. They started on one end of the long, open building and followed the plywood through all the processes required for it to emerge in sturdy square sheets. It was a long, involved operation, much more so than Carrie had imagined. Fortunately, Kevin was by her side explaining each step as they moved through the plant.

It was noon when they shed their coveralls along with the thin layer of sawdust that had settled on them and again stepped out into the cold. "If you don't have to be back right away, come to my office for lunch," Kevin suggested. "I have a small refrigerator where I keep sandwich material and drinks."

"Thank you. I'd like that. I have to be back by one, though."

"No problem," Kevin said, taking her arm and hurrying her toward the office building.

"Are Josh's offices in that larger brick building over there?" Carrie asked, gesturing, as they neared their destination.

Kevin's glance was quizzical. "Yes. Haven't you been there?"

Wishing she had not made the answer so embarrassingly obvious, Carrie said, "Not yet. Mike keeps me at home most of the time."

Back in Kevin's paneled office, he made fresh coffee and ham sandwiches generously layered with crisp pickle chips and lettuce. He brought out paper plates and cups and arranged them on a tiny table which sat in one corner with two chairs.

"You're very good at this," Carrie told him as she took her seat.

"Alas," he said with a wry smile, "my culinary ability doesn't extend much beyond coffee and sandwiches. I eat out most of the time."

"Ethel tells me there are one or two ladies around who would like to take over those domestic chores. Are you serious about anyone?"

He looked at her over the sandwich, which he held in both hands. "I'm not ready for marriage yet, if that's what you mean. I'm concentrating on my career right now."

"You seem to have done quite well," Carrie remarked, glancing about the well-furnished office.

He shrugged, hesitated, then said carefully, "The position as Josh's assistant is still open, even though his brother has been dead for over a year."

"Have you told Josh you're interested?" Carrie inquired in a noncommittal tone.

He laughed shortly. "That's hardly necessary. The problem is I'm not the only one."

"I see."

His expression was rueful. "I'm sorry. I really didn't mean to put you on the spot. Josh isn't the kind of man who mixes business with his home life, anyway."

"No." Nor would she have the slightest influence on him if he were, Carrie thought. It occurred to her that Kevin might have much more luck gaining Jessica Thorpe's ear.

She was relieved when Kevin turned the conversation to something else. They had finished eating and were having a second cup of coffee when a light tap sounded at the door and Josh walked in.

"Sorry to appear unannounced, but your secretary's out—" He halted as his eyes raked the room and fell on Carrie. He stood there, scowling, as Kevin got to his feet, obviously flustered by the censorious look on his employer's face.

"I've been showing your wife through the plant," he said, "and we came back here for—coffee. Would you like a cup?"

"No, thank you." Josh's cold gaze had not left Carrie's face.

Her cheeks felt warm as she reached for her jacket which was hanging over the back of her chair. "I'm scheduled to work a booth at the bazaar," she said hastily, slipping into the jacket and pulling it together in front, for she felt suddenly chilled. "Thanks for the tour, Kevin." She walked toward the door, passing by Josh with a quick glance. "See you at home, Josh."

Abruptly, he gripped her arm. "I'll walk you outside." When they had reached her car, he turned to her and said furiously, "What are you doing here?"

"Kevin told you," she replied, pulling free of his grip. "I had some time to pass and took him up on his offer to show me around. I—I have to go now, Josh. I promised Julia Freemont."

"You made some promises to me, too—our wedding vows," he said through gritted teeth. "Or have you forgotten?"

"I would hardly forget one of the darkest occasions of my life!" Carrie wrenched open the car door and slid into the driver's seat.

Josh held the door, preventing her from closing it. "We haven't finished this discussion," he said tensely. "I'll see you tonight." Then he slammed the door and walked back toward the office building.

Carrie drove away, her hands on the steering wheel shaking. Back at the Community Building, she welcomed the constant stream of customers at the bakery booth. Business was so good, in fact, that Julia stayed on through the afternoon to help her, introducing Carrie to dozens of people. They all treated her with warmth, talking and joking as if they had known her for years. Carrie thought that, under other circumstances, she might come to love living there.

"You're a hit," Julia told her as they were having coffee during one of the afternoon lulls in business.

"What do you mean?"

"Everybody likes you. You come across as a friendly, ordinary sort of woman who doesn't put herself in a class above common folk."

Carrie laughed. "Why should I, Julia? My background is about as ordinary and common as they come."

Julia nodded. "I don't know where Josh found you, but it was the best thing that ever happened to him. After all his problems with Helen—" She seemed abruptly to realize what she was saying and turned to pour herself more coffee. "When am I going to get to meet Mike?"

"I'll bring him down to your shop one day soon," Carrie replied, but her mind was still on what Julia had started to say. Josh and Helen had had problems—that much had slipped out before Julia caught herself. All at once, Carrie recalled something Josh had said to her in Boise: *I assure you I have few illusions about marriage.* She had wondered at the time what he meant, and Julia had inadvertently thrown a little light on that enigmatic statement. What sort of problems had he had with Helen? Carrie wondered. But she couldn't ask Julia, who probably wouldn't tell her, anyway. Nor Ethel. No, if she wished to know more on that subject, she would have to get it from Josh. And that wasn't likely to happen either, since, when he talked to her at all, it was more often than not to criticize her.

That evening was one of the rare occasions since their marriage when Josh was home for dinner. They ate with Ethel in the dining room while Betty fed Mike in the kitchen. Josh passed the entire meal in silence except when Ethel directed a question to him. Ethel would have had to be extremely dense not to realize that Josh was angry with his wife about something. As soon as she could, she excused herself to go to her apartment.

When Ethel was gone, Josh let his gaze rest unwaveringly on Carrie, the craggy angles of his face appearing harder than ever. Knowing that he had only waited until they were alone to attack her again about her visit to Kevin's office, Carrie excused herself and left the table, going up the stairs to her bedroom. Betty would be bringing Mike up any minute, and since Josh knew that, surely he wouldn't follow her.

She was wrong. She had only been in the room long enough to undress and put on a robe, preparatory to running a bath for herself, when Josh came in.

"Did you think I could be put off so easily?"

"I don't want to hear any more of your silly accusations," Carrie said as decisively as she could manage. But she found that her knees felt weak and sat down on the side of the bed. "Betty will be bringing Mike up before long."

"Not until I tell her to," Josh announced as he walked across the room and took a stand with his back to one of the large windows. "I asked her to keep Mike downstairs."

Carrie stared at him across the length of the room, feeling as a butterfly must feel when he is caught in a net. "Say what you came to say, then."

"I want you to stay away from Kevin Hamilton. You are not to see him alone again." The eyes that looked at her were colder and angrier than she had ever seen them. "I will not tolerate even a hint of gossip about my wife and another man."

"You have no right to ask that of me," she got out jerkily, making a helpless gesture. "I—I will go insane here if I can't even have friends. Most of the time I see only Mike and your mother. You certainly seem to have other things to do and places to be."

"I was not aware," he said coldly, "that you had any desire for my company."

"I—I don't—" Carrie supposed, from his point of view, he might have reason to be suspicious of her friendship with another man, but she was at the end of her emotional rope. "I'm glad to have more time with Mike, but the constant company of a ten-month-old baby isn't enough, Josh. And I refuse to allow you to tell me who my friends can be."

He regarded her for a long, silent moment, standing with his long, muscular legs spread, hands behind his back. "Since you bring it up, I've been meaning to speak to you about Mike. I've hired a nurse for him. She's had years of experience as a pediatric nurse and a governess. She'll be here next week."

Carrie gasped. "I know what you are trying to do! You want to make Mike emotionally dependent on somebody else!"

"There is not a grain of truth in that," he stated bluntly. "I have to be out of town several times a year and I will want you to go with me."

Feeling as if the world were crashing in on her, Carrie buried her face in her hands. "In heaven's name, why?"

"You are my wife, Carrie," he went on in the same cool, level voice. "I want you to act as hostess when I entertain business associates in other places."

She lifted her head to glare at him furiously. "Is that really why you married me, Josh, to get a hostess for your business meetings? Wouldn't Jessica Thorpe have been better suited to that role?"

With a savage oath, he bowed his head for a moment. Then he strode violently across the room and, sitting down beside her, pulled her against him and silenced her indignant mouth with his own.

Carrie wrenched her mouth free. "Is that your answer to all arguments?" she said breathlessly.

He pushed her back on the bed, the weight of his body pressing her down. "Let's stop talking," he growled. Then he was kissing her again, very thoroughly and quite brutally, dark anger driving him.

She did not even try to fight him; she knew it was useless. Against the demand of his lips and hands she was defenseless. Her arms went slowly about his shoulders, her fingers moving over the strong muscles at the back of his neck and stroking the silky smoothness of his hair. Somewhere inside her a small wanton voice was urging her to slip her hands inside his shirt, to feel the hard muscles of his chest and back under her hands.

He lifted his head to stare down at her, and although the angles of his face were still set in a scowl, she sensed that his anger was draining away and being replaced by the dark burning power that she saw in the depths of his eyes. Slowly his body moved off her and he was standing beside the bed, tossing aside his jacket and tie, unbuttoning his shirt, unbuckling his belt. All the while, the passionate gold-flecked eyes never left her face, as if he had undertaken to commit every line of it to memory.

Bewildered, Carrie could not summon the strength to move, or even to want to. She closed her eyes for a moment, and then it was too late, for the hard length of his naked body stretched itself beside her. When he bent to her again, his kiss, his touch, had become infinitely patient and gentle. His lips just brushed hers, then moved on to savor the curve of her cheek, the wing of her brow, her half-closed eyes.

Such new and unexpected tenderness was her final undoing. She did not even protest when his hand loosed her belt and spread her robe, then moved rhythmically over the silken curves of her body.

His mouth parted her lips with confident possession as he guided her expertly toward a sensual arousal that she had never known existed before. She felt no shame at all that her rounded breasts were straining against his hard chest seeking a new fulfillment. Her senses swam as, for long moments, his mouth and hands explored the secrets of her body, and she sensed that he was holding himself back with a great effort.

Then he made a thick, groaning sound deep in his

throat, and with an urgency he could no longer deny he pressed her back against the bed. Having lost all rational thought, Carrie yielded her body to his with total abandonment. There was momentary pain, but it was quickly forgotten in the rioting pleasure of her senses.

Chapter Six

Afterward, as the waves of passion subsided, Carrie was enfolded by an intense confusion that penetrated her sated lethargy like a cold, sharp knife. As the first sobering awareness of what she had allowed to happen swept over her, she was filled with contempt—for Josh and for herself. He was too clever for her, too experienced in the art of seduction. And she was weaker than she had imagined.

What was there in the cruel, ruthless man who lay beside her that could make her conscious of every nerve and sensation in her body, that could make her throb with her own sexuality? For the first time she knew the sensual depths to which her body could plunge, and the knowledge frightened her. She did not love Josh—she did not even like him—and yet he had this strong, primitive power over her.

Unable to keep the bitter regret within her, she was aware of the hot tears pricking at her closed eyelids.

Pressing the back of her hand over her eyes, she felt the tears begin to trickle out from beneath her lashes. Beside her, Josh stirred and she heard his abrupt voice.

"Carrie, what's wrong?"

"Everything," she murmured, her throat thick with the pain of self-loathing.

"Don't be a fool!" His voice was hardening. "Everything is right for the first time since our marriage."

Unable to speak, Carrie moved her head from side to side. Was he really that shallow? Could he go back and forth from his wife to Jessica—and who knew how many others?—without the slightest compunction? Did he really think sex would make their twisted relationship all right?

"Carrie." She could hear his impatience. "Don't make a tragic production of this. Stop acting like a child. At least have the consideration to tell me why you have suddenly dissolved into tears."

She opened her eyes and turned her head to stare through the watery mist into his angry face. "You can't rest until you've taken everything away from me, can you? First I had to marry you and bring Mike here. I am not even allowed to choose my own friends. You are bringing in a nurse to complete the job of weaning away Mike's affection and dependence on me. Now you have violated my body—"

"Violated!" There was furious scorn in the word. "Come on, Carrie! You were as eager for what happened as I was. You can't be self-deceiving enough to believe otherwise, nor can I understand why you would want to believe it. I *was* considerate enough to marry you before taking you to bed."

"Oh, yes!" she declared scathingly. "You are so considerate that you are stealing everything I hold dear, and you expect me to like it when you—when you take unfair advantage of a situation. It was rape, Josh."

Icy contempt glazed his eyes, but she was too emotionally drained to feel more than a depressing indifference.

"Why must you lie to yourself?" he inquired witheringly. "Marriage should not be a battleground."

"I do not know what marriage should be," she retorted. "I have never had a real one." Gathering the remnants of her pride, she turned abruptly away from him, drawing up her knees to her chest and hugging herself against the chill that came from deep inside her.

With a jerking movement, Josh sat up and away from her. Uttering a string of oaths, he snatched up his shirt and shrugged into it with intolerant haste. Then, picking up the remainder of his clothes, he left her to go to his own suite.

When he was gone, Carrie moved shakily from the bed. Gazing down at her tender, pale nakedness, she felt a resurgence of her earlier bewilderment, as if she had somehow found herself in another woman's body. Her lips parted in disbelief as she recalled the last hour in Josh's arms. Now, however, instead of her body feeling aglow with heat, it was trembling with a chill. She could guess where Josh would be going as soon as he had dressed, and the episode just past seemed degradingly sordid. In spite of what she had said to Josh, she knew that she was not without blame in what had happened, and she felt sick with shame.

But life had to go on. She decided to put off her bath and moved hastily to dress and go down to the kitchen. She did not want to be alone. She would bring Mike up and let him play for as long as he wanted in his bath. If Josh went ahead with his plan to bring a nurse into the house, Carrie would probably have few opportunities in the future to spend long, uninterrupted hours with the baby.

She did not really have any hope that her objections would change Josh's mind, and she was right not to hope. On the day before Thanksgiving, the nurse arrived. Mike was napping and Carrie was having a cup of tea with Ethel in her apartment when Josh appeared with a small, birdlike woman in tow. Her thin, graying brown hair was cut extremely short with bangs across her forehead, and she wore a sensible brown gabardine suit and even more sensible brown oxfords.

"Mother, Carrie, I want you to meet Emily Hastings. Miss Hastings has come to take charge of Mike."

Miss Hastings greeted them amiably enough but refused to accept tea. Carrie had the feeling that the nurse thought it would be out of place to take tea with the mistresses of the house.

After a few moments of conversation, in which Carrie took no part, Josh took Miss Hastings upstairs to the bedroom that had been prepared for her with a connecting door to the one that had been turned into Mike's nursery.

Carrie had objected to Josh that there was plenty of room in her suite for Mike and his things, but her husband remained adamant that the baby should have a room of his own. "Let him have a little breathing space, Carrie," Josh had said to her. "Don't smother him as Mother did Danny."

Highly insulted by the comparison, Carrie had barely spoken to him in the past two days. He had, in his usual imperious manner, gone ahead with preparations for the nurse. Somewhat to Carrie's disappointment, Mike had not fretted over being moved away from her. In fact, he had taken great delight in exploring his new quarters and had even ventured to take a few steps unaided across the nursery floor.

Mike was allowed to share the lavish Thanksgiving dinner in the dining room with the rest of the family. Seeming to sense the importance of the occasion, the baby laughed and babbled between hearty bites of the delicious food, while the nurse hovered anxiously nearby in case he should drop anything on the carpet. The final insult to Carrie came when Josh offered Mike more mashed potatoes and the little boy looked up, eyes brimming with good spirits, and announced, "Daddy!"

This was too much to swallow, and Carrie soon excused herself to go into one of the sitting rooms where a log fire blazed. She was still sitting and staring broodingly into the fire when Ethel joined her.

"Josh has gone out for a walk."

Carrie uttered an uninterested sound, and Ethel sat down on the couch near her. After a moment of silence, the older woman said, "Carrie, I'm not trying to intrude into your personal life, but is there anything I can do to help settle this thing between you and Josh?"

Carrie looked over at her with a blank expression. "What thing?"

"My dear, I'm not blind. Something is wrong between the two of you. What has Josh done to anger you?"

Carrie had a momentarily strong impulse to open her mouth and let everything spill out. *Your son is a selfish, unfeeling monster who is determined to have his way, no matter how many other people are hurt. He has forced, tormented, and bullied me to the limit of my endurance, and if it weren't for Mike I'd have left here long ago.* Only the imagined picture of Ethel's kind, sweet face paling with shock stopped her.

"I don't think Mike needs a nurse," she said finally.

Ethel nodded sadly. "I thought that might be it.

Carrie, the way you have loved and cared for that baby is heartwarming. I know it must have been extremely trying for you, losing your sister and then suddenly finding yourself with the complete care of a baby on your hands. Clearly, the father was no help to you."

"I don't want to discuss it," Carrie said quietly.

"Of course you don't," Ethel commiserated, her voice warm with compassion. "Nor do I want you to. I'm merely trying to help you see Josh's point of view. He realizes, as I do, how hard it has been on you, raising Mike—not that you didn't want to. Now that you are Josh's wife, let him lift some of that burden from you."

Carrie pushed the heavy weight of her hair off her forehead in a weary gesture. "Mother, I never thought of caring for Mike as a burden."

"I'm saying this very badly," Ethel apologized. "It's just that I know, from personal experience, that sometimes a mother can become too emotionally dependent on a child. So much so that, with all the love and good intentions in the world, she can create a situation that isn't good for the child."

"Are you saying I've done that with Mike?"

"No." Ethel's blue eyes were sympathetic as they surveyed her. "But I think Josh fears that might happen. You see, he disapproved of the way I coddled Danny. He tried several times to talk to me about it, but I wouldn't listen. I didn't want to believe that I was harming my son, but I was forced to realize what I had been doing when Danny began to rebel. I—I think sometimes that he was still rebelling when he insisted that Josh send him to South Africa, and perhaps even when he drove that sports car so recklessly that he lost his life."

Carrie's pity went out to the older woman, the sadness in Ethel's blue eyes now wringing her heart. "I don't believe that for a moment," she said earnestly. "People have to be responsible for their own actions. Whatever Danny did, *he* did it, not you."

Ethel sighed. "I know. I do, really. I'm only trying to explain Josh's feelings to you. Mike is very important to him. I confess that I am sometimes amazed at this new paternal side of him, and yet I think I can understand it. When he lost Helen—well, it was bad enough to lose his wife, but to lose his child, too—"

"His *child?*" Carrie gazed with incredulity at her mother-in-law.

"I see my suspicion is correct. He hasn't told you about the baby, has he? Well, it's no more than I expected. Josh doesn't talk easily about such things. But in this case I think he is wrong to keep it all inside. You see, Helen was pregnant when she died in that hotel fire."

Carrie shook her head slowly. "No, I didn't know. Josh has never said a word to me about Helen or—the way she died."

"If he knows that I have told you this, he will probably be angry with me. But I want so much to help, Carrie. I want this marriage to work."

"Thank you, Mother," Carrie got out. "You needn't worry that I'll repeat to Josh what you have told me."

"If ever you think it would help your relationship, I want you to tell him," Ethel said stoutly. "There shouldn't be any secrets between husband and wife."

Later, alone in her bedroom, Carrie recalled with some wonderment that conversation with Ethel. For the first time she began to understand why Mike was so important to Josh. It wasn't just that he was Danny's child. Mike was evidently the son Josh might have had with Helen if that fire had never happened, or if Helen hadn't been staying in that hotel. This was, in fact, something that had puzzled Carrie several times. Why had Helen gone to Toronto alone? If she'd had family there she wouldn't have been staying in a hotel. Had it been a vacation that Josh had been too busy to share with her? Now that she knew Helen had been pregnant, that seemed somehow unlikely. At least, Carrie could not imagine herself pregnant and leaving a husband she loved for a vacation in a Toronto hotel. But Julia Freemont had said that Josh and Helen had had problems. Maybe Helen had gone away to try to think through those problems.

In spite of everything that had passed between her and Josh, Carrie discovered that she could feel sorry for him. Whatever his problems with his first wife, he must have suffered terribly when she and their baby died. More perhaps than Carrie had suffered when Meg died. She had had Mike to make up, in part, for the loss, while Josh had had nothing.

By now she knew all of the ways in which Josh was to blame for their situation. But she wondered if she had been unfair in her sweeping assessment of him as totally selfish and cruel. He did seem to love Mike.

It was with these thoughts again in her mind that she arrived in the kitchen early the next morning to join Mike for breakfast. She was greeted by Betty's approving smile. "You are joining Mr. Josh for breakfast in the dining room? How nice. I'll set another place."

Before Carrie could protest that it was Mike she had come to see, Betty was hurrying from the kitchen with plate, silver, and napkin. Adam Carney was at the stove pouring coffee into a big mug. "Hasn't Miss Hastings brought Mike down yet?" Carrie asked him.

"She asked to have his breakfast served in the nursery," Adam told her.

Carrie was tempted to have her breakfast taken up to the nursery, too, but it would be too awkward to try to explain to Betty why she refused to eat with Josh. Sighing, she made her way to the dining room.

Josh, in white shirt and tie, looked up at her entrance

with a wry smile. "Betty thinks it's considerate of you to come down so early just to have breakfast with me." His look was mocking. "I didn't disillusion her by telling her your reason for coming down was undoubtedly much less romantic. Hoping to eat with Mike, weren't you?"

Carrie took her seat at his right, where Betty had arranged her place setting. "Yes, but his nurse is feeding him upstairs."

"You can see him there any time you wish."

"With the starched Miss Hastings crackling in the background?"

"If you'll give her a chance, Carrie, I think you'll come to appreciate her. She's very good with Mike. Of course, you can take Mike to your suite or anywhere else any time you want."

"As long as I don't interfere with Miss Hastings' schedule?"

He eyed her thoughtfully. "You know a schedule is important with young children. But Emily Hastings is only Mike's nurse. You're his mother."

Carrie's eyes widened in mock astonishment. "I was sure you had forgotten that!"

"Still haven't forgiven me for hiring a nurse, have you? Are you continuing to blame me for—other things?"

The narrowed brown eyes glinted with a suggestive meaning, and somehow Carrie knew he was remembering the occasion, a week ago now, when they had come together with such explosive passion, The knowledge triggered a fierce heat that moved up her neck and flushed her cheeks. Desperate to turn the direction of his thoughts, she said hastily, "There are sales in most of the stores in town today. I thought I'd start shopping for Christmas presents."

He looked amused. "This penchant of yours to pinch pennies is commendable, I'm sure, but you seem to forget you don't have to live on quite such a strict budget now. You haven't even bought any new clothes since our marriage."

Disconcerted, she retorted, "I see no reason to waste money, even if it is available. You married a woman who has always had to be careful with money. You can't expect me to change the habits of a lifetime and suddenly start throwing money away. I'm sorry if my wardrobe isn't elaborate enough for you, Josh, but I am what I am." This last was said with a note of defiance.

Josh merely finished his egg, leaned back in his chair, and said calmly, "Don't be so defensive, Carrie. I'm not complaining." He was watching her, the gold-flecked eyes shaded by thick lashes. Yet the look was enervating, and Carrie stirred uncomfortably in her chair.

"I—I was hoping you might have some ideas about a Christmas present for your mother. I know she likes antiques, but I know so little about what is authentic in that line that I've no idea what to look for."

"I'll try to learn something from Mother without making her suspicious," Josh said. "In the meantime, you might ask Jessica for some ideas. She's something of an authority on antiques."

Among other things, Carrie thought darkly. She kept her opinion to herself, but she didn't promise to ask Jessica's advice. When Josh left for the office, she finished her breakfast quickly and went upstairs to spend some time with Mike, sending Miss Hastings downstairs for a coffee break. The nurse seemed glad enough to leave the baby in Carrie's hands and asked when Carrie would like her to return. Carrie named a time an hour away and the birdlike woman left without further comment, making it unnecessary for Carrie to deliver the stern lecture she had been preparing in case the nurse opposed her. It seemed that Emily Hastings knew her place, and Carrie was relieved.

The hour with Mike was enjoyable. Upon the nurse's return, Carrie went to her bedroom for her coat, which she put on over tan slacks and sweater. Stopping by Ethel's apartment, she asked if the older woman needed anything from town. Ethel replied negatively, bidding Carrie to have a good time on her shopping trip.

The small town was decorated for the season with lighted stars and wreaths strung across the main streets and shopwindows full of Christmas displays. Carrie spent a leisurely couple of hours browsing in the shops and buying a few items: clothes and a rocking horse for Mike, which the shop proprietor promised to deliver on Christmas Eve; costume jewelry for Gracie; a beautiful hand-painted shawl for Betty; and fur-lined gloves for Adam.

Shopping for Josh was more difficult. She finally purchased a handmade wallet and silk shirts, leaving both wallet and shirts to be imprinted with Josh's initials. She would, she promised herself, find something else before Christmas. Ethel's gift was the only one she hadn't bought, and Carrie was still pondering this problem as she entered a small café for lunch. Too late she noticed Jessica Thorpe alone at a table. Before she could retreat Jessica looked up and saw her.

"Come share my table," the black-haired woman called to her.

Reluctantly, Carrie crossed the café and took a chair facing Jessica. Eyeing her shopping bag, Jessica commented, "Doing some shopping, I see."

"I picked up a few Christmas gifts."

After they had given their order to a waitress, Jessica asked perfunctory questions about Ethel and Mike. Then: "Josh tells me the baby has a new nurse."

Carrie nodded, unwilling to comment, but Jessica evidently saw the disapproval on her face. "You don't like her?"

Forced to reply, Carrie said, "I neither like nor dislike Emily. I don't really know her."

"Then it must be the whole idea of Mike's having a nurse that you find distasteful," Jessica probed.

"Not distasteful," Carrie returned, "unnecessary. But then I imagine Josh has told you my feelings on the subject." Indeed, she suspected that Jessica knew a great deal about her relationship with her husband. Josh must have told her that the marriage was one of convenience, and Carrie wondered now if Josh had also told her that he'd taken Carrie to bed. Surely not, but even the thought of it made it difficult for Carrie to meet Jessica's intent brown eyes.

"Only in passing," Jessica replied somewhat carefully. "I've seen him several times lately, but we usually talk about other things."

Carrie felt sure this was meant to provoke jealous curiosity, but she refused to be baited. When their lunch arrived, she turned her attention to the food, merely replying tersely to Jessica's conversational gambits. Finally the other woman remarked ironically, "You seem preoccupied, Carrie. I'd better be off, anyway. I've a lot to accomplish this afternoon, and I'm expecting Josh to come by when he leaves the office." The brown eyes grew wide then, as if she had said more than she intended, and she added, "On a business matter. I hope you don't mind my delaying his arrival home this evening."

"I never interfere in my husband's *business*," Carrie said shortly.

After Jessica had gone, Carrie realized that every muscle in her body was rigid with tension. She made a conscious effort to relax as she drank a second cup of coffee. She shouldn't let Jessica Thorpe's veiled insinuations ruffle her so. After all, she had always suspected that Josh was carrying on an affair with the woman, a relationship that had begun long before her marriage to

Josh. Perhaps she was disappointed because, since Ethel's disclosure the day before, she had been feeling a little sorry for Josh. Clearly her sympathy was misplaced. Why she should feel hurt by having her suspicions confirmed she didn't know. In fact, she was angry with herself for feeling anything at all.

She was still feeling cross when Josh, who had missed dinner again, came to her bedroom that evening to say he had to go to Boise on business for a few days.

"Would you like to come with me?"

Carrie had been sitting in an armchair reading a magazine, and with his appearance she felt her body stiffen. "No, thank you," she said. "I don't think I should leave Mike at this time."

Josh made a gesture of impatience. "Mike is in good hands. One of the purposes for hiring a nurse was so that you would be free to accompany me on these trips."

"It's too soon," Carrie said. "Mike hasn't had time to get used to Miss Hastings yet. Besides, earlier today he acted as though he were coming down with a cold."

"He's as healthy as a horse," retorted Josh. "You're merely making excuses, Carrie, and not very convincing ones at that. I want you to come to Boise with me."

Her blue-green eyes sparked angrily. "Well, *I* don't want to come. You can't force me, Josh, unless you intend to tie me up and carry me onto the plane."

Standing over her, he gazed at her from narrowed eyes, his mouth turning down in anger. "I'm tempted, Carrie," he said harshly, "but suddenly your company doesn't seem at all desirable." With that, he turned on his heel and left her.

Trembling from the encounter, Carrie let the magazine slip to the floor and held her head in her hands. Would he take Jessica with him? she wondered and discovered that she resented the idea enormously.

Chapter Seven

Two evenings later, Carrie was seated in a local restaurant across a candlelit table from Kevin Hamilton. "This is nice," she said. "I needed to get out of the house."

He had come by that afternoon with some business papers to be given to Josh upon his return from Boise. Insisting that he have a cup of coffee with her in the sitting room, Carrie had expressed regret at not having seen him since their tour of the plywood plant.

Kevin had hesitated for a moment, then said, "I wasn't sure Josh would approve."

Meeting his gaze steadily, Carrie had said, "I choose my own friends, Kevin."

He had surprised her then by inviting her to have dinner with him. She had accepted the invitation readily, and even Ethel had voiced approval when Carrie informed her of her intention of having dinner with Kevin. "It's considerate of him to help you pass the time while Josh is away," Ethel had commented with her usual optimistic disregard for the objections of more small-minded people. Apparently it never occurred to her that Josh wouldn't like it.

Sitting across from Kevin now, Carrie told herself there was no reason for Josh even to find out about the dinner. But if he did, she assured herself, she didn't care.

Kevin smiled at her. "You're very attractive in blue. That outfit was made for you."

She glanced down at the suit she had purchased for her wedding, then returned his smile. "Coming from you, that's high praise." She ran her eyes approvingly over his cashmere sports jacket, which, like all his clothes, fitted perfectly.

Kevin raised his brow as he looked at her. "How am I to take that?"

"I mean that you have excellent taste in clothes. You always look as if you stepped from the pages of *Esquire*."

He inclined his head slightly in acknowledgment. "Believe me, living in this out-of-the-way place makes it difficult to keep up with fashion."

Carrie suppressed a smile. Kevin really was something of a dandy. Clearly his wardrobe was one of his top priorities. She couldn't help comparing him with Josh, who, although he dressed well, often seemed unaware of what he was wearing, as if clothes were only an unimportant but necessary part of life. Even though he encouraged Carrie to buy clothing for herself and Mike, she had noticed that he put off shopping for himself.

Carrie relaxed in the intimate atmosphere of the restaurant and listened to Kevin talk about his job with the Revell Corporation. As they were starting dessert,

Jessica Thorpe came in with another woman, and the change in Kevin's manner was obvious.

Jessica merely nodded toward their table before disappearing into another dining room. After she was out of sight, Kevin continued to shift uneasily in his chair, and although Carrie tried to pick up their conversation again, it was clear that his mind was no longer on what he had been telling her.

"What's wrong, Kevin?" she asked finally. "I get the feeling I'm talking to a wall."

He toyed with his fork and glanced up at her. "Doesn't it bother you, being seen here with me by Jessica Thorpe?"

Carrie had been a little unsettled by Jessica's appearance, but she pushed down the feeling. Surprisingly, stronger than her worry over Josh's reaction was the relief she felt in the certain knowledge that Jessica had not gone to Boise with Josh. Until that moment, she hadn't been sure and hadn't known how to go about finding out.

"Why should it bother me?"

"I should think you might be concerned over what your husband will think." He shrugged. "Maybe you're sure enough of his trust that you don't have to be concerned, but he's my employer."

"I didn't mean to make light of your loyalty to Josh," Carrie assured him. "We are just two friends having dinner. We aren't doing anything wrong, so don't worry."

Kevin gave her an odd sort of look that made Carrie wonder, all at once, if he had thought this evening might lead to something more than friendship. But she cast the thought aside quickly, telling herself that Jessica's unexpected appearance was making her too sensitive. Whatever Kevin might have thought, however, his concern over being seen by Jessica caused him to be moody and withdrawn after that. Carrie was just

as glad to get back to the Revell house as she had been
to leave it a short while earlier.

For the first few days after Josh returned from Boise,
Carrie was cautious every time they were alone together, expecting angry recriminations about her dinner
with Kevin. The dreaded confrontation did not materi-
alize, however. Though she couldn't help wondering
why Jessica had let such an ideal opportunity for
undermining Josh's faith in her go by, she was vastly
relieved.

Several heavy snowfalls blanketed the area as De-
cember progressed. As a result, Carrie found it more
difficult to get into town. Josh went to his office every
day, of course, but he was much more accustomed to
driving over snow-packed roads than Carrie was.
Mostly she stayed in the house, spending long hours
with Mike and Ethel. Miss Hastings continued to be
retiring and never opposed any plans Carrie made
for the baby. Had she been on better terms with her
husband, Carrie might have confessed to him she was
beginning to think her fears concerning the nurse had
been unnecessary. But she saw little of Josh. He
frequently stayed late at the office, or so he said. Carrie
was certain that some of his evenings were spent with
Jessica.

When Josh informed her that they would be attend-
ing the country club dinner-dance a few evenings
before Christmas, Carrie actually looked forward to it
and made plans to go into town to buy a new gown for
the occasion.

She was so eager to be out that the next morning
when she awoke feeling somewhat ill, she climbed out
of bed anyway, fighting nausea, and dressed in warm
slacks, sweater, and boots. Mike had had a mild case of
the sniffles, and she decided she had caught his bug.
Taking several deep breaths to still her churning

stomach, she marched out of her bedroom and descended the stairs. In the kitchen she forced down a piece of toast and a few sips of hot tea, then went to tell Ethel that she would be out for the morning.

By the time she was in her car, which was newly equipped with snow tires, and leaving the Revell estate behind, she began to feel better. The tea seemed to have settled her stomach, and she drove the five miles to town without any trouble.

Trudging from one shop to another, she took inventory of the formal dresses available in town. There weren't many, and she was beginning to think her old velvet skirt and silk blouse would have to do for the country club when she found the perfect gown. Made of clinging burgundy Qiana, the halter top dipped to a V between her breasts, leaving her back bare almost to the waist. The skirt clung to her hips, then fell to the floor in soft folds which caught the light. The gown fit perfectly, and when the salesgirl showed her a pair of spike-heeled shoes the same burgundy shade as the dress, Carrie wrote out a check for both. The figure was staggering, but, remembering that Josh could well afford it, she smiled as she handed the girl the check.

Josh didn't see the gown until she descended the stairs on the evening of the dinner-dance and entered the sitting room where they had set up the huge Christmas tree. He turned at the sound of the soft swish of her skirt.

In a black dinner jacket and ruffle-fronted white shirt, he looked devastatingly handsome as his eyes widened, then narrowed and ran over her. "Well." His tone held satisfaction. "You will certainly be the most beautiful woman there tonight."

"Thank you," she said in a soft voice. "You like my new gown, then?"

"*Like* is hardly adequate to express my opinion of your gown, my dear," he said rather dryly.

Feeling at a loss how to react to that, Carrie said, "I'll get my coat."

"Wait." Josh strode to the brightly decorated tree and lifted a large package from the pile underneath. "Open this before we go."

"Won't we be late?"

Ignoring her protest, he put the box into her hands. She sat down on the couch and tore off the wrappings. When she pushed back the layers of tissue to expose a mink evening jacket, a sudden feeling of unreality came over her. Gingerly she ran her fingers over the luxurious fur, quite unable to speak.

Then Josh was bending over her, lifting the jacket from its box. "Let's see if I guessed your size correctly."

She stood and allowed him to slide the jacket up her arms and pull it over her shoulders. Standing behind her, his hands cupping the warm collar against her neck, he said in a quiet voice, "The fit is fine. Do you like it?"

"It's lovely." Carrie was amazed to feel a knot of tears gathering in her throat. No doubt it was the shock. What was Josh up to now? She swallowed hard and walked over to view her reflection in a wall mirror. The jacket was a rich brown very near the color of her hair, reaching just below her waist, with a short stand-up collar. She could hardly believe that *she* was the elegant-looking woman who stared back at her.

"I never saw anything as—as glamorous as this jacket, Josh. Thank you."

He came up behind her, and for a moment their gazes caught in the mirror. Carrie thought that he was going to touch her and, perversely, felt disappointment when he merely said, "Shall we go?"

The country club was situated on the other side of town from the Revell estate. Josh at the wheel of the Mercedes handled the snowy roads with ease. Their conversation during the drive centered on Mike, the fact that he was beginning to walk everywhere, and the presents Carrie had bought him for Christmas.

With Josh beside her, Carrie felt an uncharacteristic self-confidence as they entered the country club building. It was with some reluctance that she left her jacket in the cloakroom, as if she feared she might shed her confidence with the mink.

They found the dining room already filled as they entered. One of the first couples to come into Carrie's line of vision was Jessica Thorpe and a distinguished-looking white-haired gentleman who was gazing down at her with an adoring smile.

Seeing the direction of her look, Josh said, "That's Emmet Travis. He owns several hotels across the river in Washington. He was a friend of Jessie's late husband."

Although he must be twenty years older than Jessica, Travis was still a handsome man, and clearly wealthy. He seemed to exude the aura of money.

His hand on her arm, Josh was steering Carrie toward a table where the McCloys and Kevin Hamilton were already seated. Greetings were exchanged, and Christine turned to Carrie. "You look as pretty as a picture, honey." Her auburn curls bounced as she tilted her head to one side. "That dress is a knockout, and you've got the figure for it."

"Thank you." Carrie's confidence took another lift, but it was short-lived, for Jessica and her escort were approaching the table. Jessica wore a stunning, figure-hugging silver gown stitched all over with metallic strands that glistened provocatively with every move she made. She accepted the chorus of greetings and admiring glances with tolerant amusement, but her brown eyes deepened with a sensual glow and a flicker of possessiveness as she glanced at Josh.

"Josh, darling!" she purred as she swept around the

table, followed by Emmet Travis, one elegant hand coming to rest on the black sleeve of Josh's dinner jacket. "There is something I must discuss with you."

As Josh smiled slightly and moved to assist Jessica into the chair next to his, Carrie caught Christine's look. Christine's eyes seemed to say, "You haven't a chance against her," and Carrie experienced a strange desire to prove Christine wrong, a desire she instantly commanded herself to ignore.

"We'll talk later, Jessie," Josh said, his expression unfathomable as he looked across at Carrie. Emmet Travis was now seated on Jessica's other side. "Emmet," Josh said, "may I introduce my wife, Carrie? Carrie, this is Emmet Travis."

"How do you do, my dear." Sharply etched lips parted in a smile that revealed even white teeth, but there was a trace of sympathy in the light blue eyes as they swept over Carrie.

Jessica, who seemed to have noticed Carrie for the first time, took in the burgundy gown with amusement. "Josh, darling, you must allow your wife to go to Seattle, or at least Boise, for her clothes. That dress has been in Rena's shop for at least six months."

Carrie's chin jutted forward as Christine stifled a gasp. It was the most blatant insult Carrie had ever encountered in a social situation, and Josh apparently had no intention of coming to her rescue. Instead, he smiled lazily and raised an eyebrow for Carrie's benefit. Carrie felt her hackles rising.

"Where did you find your gown, Jessica?" she inquired in a tone as deliberately sweet as honey.

"Oh, there is an absolute prize of a designer in Seattle. She chooses her clients with care, but if I recommend you she will take you on."

"Never mind," returned Carrie. "I don't like the flashy look."

Travis glanced from one face to the other in this tense

little scene and cleared his throat. "Jessie always makes the best-dressed lists in this part of the country."

"How nice," Carrie acknowledged coolly, her blue-green eyes still meeting Jessica's now furious look. "She probably has all the time in the world to plan her wardrobe. Most women have other responsibilities."

Jessica's dark eyes smoldered venomously, but Josh intervened with a sharp glance. "We seem to have a misunderstanding here."

"No," Carrie cut in, meeting his level gaze. "Jessica and I understand each other very well, I think."

She looked back at Jessica, head held high. She'd heard all of the woman's snide innuendoes that she cared to. Hereafter, she would strike back.

Emmet placed his hand over Jessica's and held it for a moment. "May I order you a cocktail, sweetheart?"

The tension in the air was relieved as Travis summoned a waiter, who took their orders for drinks. Then the mediating Travis caught Carrie's eyes and said, "I understand you have an adopted son."

Carrie took a deep breath and forced a smile to her cold lips. "Yes, Mr. Travis. Mike will be a year old next month. Driving here, Josh and I were talking about how fast he is growing. He recently started walking."

Their drinks arrived, followed shortly by the first course of their dinner. For Carrie it was a difficult meal to sit through. Christine McCloy and Kevin Hamilton, apparently in an effort to prevent any more antagonism from surfacing, kept up a lively conversation about recent civic events and the coming holidays. Jessica, sitting directly across from Carrie, made it all too obvious that she was bored by the conversation and repeatedly leaned over to speak quietly into Josh's ear. Josh, except for brief replies to Jessica, maintained a brooding silence. When Carrie met his glance after the first course, she received the impression that he was expecting her to attack Jessica again, perhaps more directly this time. Carrie had an impish impulse to knock the full water pitcher into Jessica's elegant lap but resisted with some difficulty.

After the five-course meal, the orchestra began playing dance melodies and Travis immediately asked Jessica to dance. Jessica's glance at the older man was impatient, but she rose from her chair, glistening, and accepted his hand. The McCloys followed them to the dance floor, and Carrie glanced at Josh, who had been drinking steadily all through the meal, his expression enigmatic. She found it impossible to guess his thoughts and turned to answer a question put to her by Kevin Hamilton.

Probably suspecting that Kevin was about to ask her to dance, Josh said abruptly, "Would you like to dance, Carrie?"

Carrie met his cold look once more with a sickening feeling in her stomach, but her expression remained veiled as she nodded silently and allowed her husband to lead her onto the dance floor. As Josh's arms came around her in a loose, impersonal embrace she asked herself why it should matter to her how Josh and Jessica behaved.

Determined not to be the first to break the stony silence, Carrie pressed her lips together. The melody was half through when Josh finally said, "Your first important social event as my wife isn't turning out very well."

She looked up at him then and saw a hardening of all his features. "I suppose you think it's my fault."

"You certainly haven't helped the situation."

"What should I have done, Josh? Sat there and allowed Jessica Thorpe to insult me?"

His gold-flecked eyes glittered down at her. "You have to know Jessie. She only meant to accommodate you when she offered to recommend you to her designer."

Carrie had begun to tremble with anger. "She meant to make me feel gauche and foolish in front of the others. I won't stand for it, Josh. I am not the least bit ashamed of my background or my wardrobe—or anything else. I have much more important things to do than to flit around town to committee meetings and traipse over to Seattle for specially designed clothes."

"Indeed?" he murmured, staring at her through narrowed eyes for a moment before shrugging carelessly. "I don't want to argue with you. As I told you earlier, you look very beautiful tonight. You needn't be envious of Jessie."

"Envious!" she exclaimed. "I feel not the slightest envy for a woman who throws herself at other women's husbands!" She turned her head to stare over his shoulder but still felt his eyes on her. She was relieved when the melody ended and they could return to the table. To her chagrin, however, Jessica and Emmet returned at the same time, and when Kevin Hamilton asked her to dance she accepted with alacrity.

When she and Kevin were moving smoothly to the music, she felt herself relaxing for the first time since she'd walked into the dining room and caught sight of Jessica. They talked easily, and she felt her composure reasserting itself. But it crumpled just as quickly when she saw Josh leading Jessica onto the dance floor. At the end of the dance, Kevin returned her to the table, but Josh and Jessica did not come back. After a few minutes, she accepted Emmet Travis's invitation to dance.

Held lightly in the older man's arms, she glanced surreptitiously about the dance floor. Josh and Jessica were no longer to be seen. Nor were they at the table when she and Emmet returned. In fact, it was several dances later when they appeared, and Jessica gave Carrie a smug look before going off to dance with Kevin.

As her introduction to the social life of the community, the evening was a disaster for Carrie. She danced again with Josh and twice more with Kevin, but it was an effort to keep up her end of the conversation, particularly with Josh, who seemed determined to drink himself under the table between dances.

By the time the evening was over, Carrie had been made to feel like an outsider who would never be accepted into the world where Josh moved so easily. During the drive home, Josh finally decided to talk.

"I hope you enjoyed your evening with Kevin Hamilton."

She glanced over at him in time to see his lips curl cynically. She remembered all too vividly her dances with Josh when he had held her rigidly, like a distant stranger, and she had experienced a perverse desire to have him press her closer. The unfairness of his attack now only served to hurt her further, but she was determined not to let him know it.

"What enjoyment there was in the evening," she said stiffly, "was in knowing that not everyone found me inappropriately dressed and boring company."

His heavy-lidded eyes appraised her with a coolness that sent an involuntary shiver up her spine. "I couldn't care less what you choose to wear, and although I have found your company many things, it is rarely boring. However, I must object to your flirtation with Kevin. I have asked you not to see him alone. You deliberately disobeyed me, not only by dancing with him tonight but by having dinner in a restaurant with him while I was in Boise."

Carrie's anger increased. He had known about her dinner with Kevin all along and had been waiting for the right moment to bring it up. "You sound like a general barking orders to a private. This is not the army, Josh! If you insist on issuing commands, I will continue to disobey as I please. Why do you want to continue this pretended marriage? Do you really want to be married to a woman who cares nothing for you?"

There was a golden gleam in the eyes that swept over her. "I am not yet convinced that we can't make a success of this. We have only been married six weeks. I once vowed that if I ever married again, it would be for good."

"That," she said uncomfortably, "was when you planned to marry Jessica. You couldn't have known that another woman would be forced upon you. But when you made a bad bargain, Josh, it's doubly foolish to keep on with it. Wouldn't it be wiser to give me a divorce and allow me to take Mike away with me? You could continue to provide for him if you wish."

His tight smile was a mockery. "I'm not ready to admit defeat yet. We will not discuss divorce. I am a determined man, Carrie."

Carrie noticed abstractedly that they had reached the estate as Josh turned the car between the stone pillars. In spite of the prodigious amount of alcohol he had consumed, he seemed in perfect command of the car. "Yes, you are determined," Carrie said angrily as they walked into the house through the back hall. "You are determined to have your cake and eat it, too!"

He glanced carelessly over his shoulder as he strode through the house with Carrie at his heels. "What is that supposed to mean?"

They had reached the foyer now, and Carrie turned to face him. "You want to keep me as some kind of salve to your pride, and you want to continue your relationship with Jessica."

His eyebrows rose sardonically. "What an imagination you have!"

"I did not imagine that you disappeared with that woman for half an hour this evening!" Carrie's voice rose shrilly.

Josh's hand shot out to grip her arm. "Keep your voice down. You'll wake Mother."

"Don't worry." Carrie controlled her voice with great difficulty. "Your mother is the only one in this family who has any human compassion and understanding. I wouldn't want her to learn what a devious devil her son is!" She jerked away from him and turned to run up the stairs. In her anger, she ran too quickly, caught the hem of her gown under her foot, and, tripping, fell to her knees on one of the carpeted stairs.

"Carrie?" As she struggled to get to her feet, she heard Josh running up the stairs behind her. Supporting her with both hands, he helped her to stand. "Are you all right?" She looked up at him, amazed at the seeming concern in his tone. How could he switch his emotions off and on so quickly? Perhaps he was drunk, after all.

She tried to pull away from him. "I'm not hurt." But she swayed against him and with an oath he swept her into his arms and carried her on up the stairs. In her bedroom, he deposited her unceremoniously on the bed, where she sat, still wearing the mink jacket, and looked up at him.

She was not prepared for the fierce anger in his eyes. "You little fool! How long are you going to keep up this running battle? You could have hurt yourself seriously just now!"

"Leave me alone, Josh. I can't stand this anymore. Go—go see Jessica. She's probably waiting for you, anyway."

"Are you quite finished?"

"No!" She tore off the jacket and threw it at him. "Take this with you. I don't want any presents from you!"

Slowly he bent to pick up the jacket from the floor at his feet. As he tossed it across the dressing table his smoldering eyes never left Carrie, who now sat hunched over. His chest heaved as he drew a deep breath to control himself. "You are the most maddeningly stubborn woman I've ever known. I told you this before, and I am more convinced of it than ever. You *enjoy* playing the martyr. I have given you my home and my name, and all you can do is sit there and feel sorry for yourself."

The accusation was too close to the truth not to sting a little, but Carrie managed to remain outwardly indifferent. "If you don't mind, I would like to go to bed."

She ran a weary hand across her forehead, but the hand stilled as he continued. "That gown looks lovely on you. You have excellent taste, and you are right— the sort of extreme fashions that Jessie wears would only take away from your natural beauty."

Bewildered by his swift change from criticism to compliment, Carrie could only stare at him speechlessly.

"It never entered my mind to leave you and go to her," he went on, seemingly unaware of how confused she felt by his abrupt change in mood. "At the moment I have no desire to be anywhere but here."

Suddenly his hands gripped her, pulling her to her feet. "Carrie—"

"Don't." She brushed off his hands, but not before she was aware, deep inside her, of the pleasurable warmth that had overcome her once before. Since that night more than four weeks ago, he had touched her only in an impersonal manner, and now she experienced the hot tingle of awareness running along all her nerves, leaving a trail of sensual desire that she struggled to fight.

The silence between them as they stood so close together was heavy with unspoken emotions.

"Are you going to fight me forever, Carrie?" he asked finally. "Is this how you want to live?"

"I—I wish I'd never met you."

The golden centers of his eyes flashed with anger. "But you did meet me, and we are married. We—are—married."

A quiver of apprehension raced through Carrie as she stared at him blankly for a moment. "I don't know what you want from me."

"Don't you?" His eyes were laden with mockery. "Then I will be more explicit. I want to share your bed, as is my right."

"Your right!" she gasped as she shrank away from him. "Don't talk to me about rights. I—I want you to go."

"I am tired of what you want." She could not move away from him as his hands came out and clamped about her wrists, pinning her arms at her sides. "Besides, I don't believe you are as indifferent to me as you pretend."

"That's not true," she breathed frantically as she tossed her hair back to glare up at him. But his return look was relentless.

"We'll see, Carrie," he said thickly, hauling her suddenly against him, his arms closing about her like two steel bands. There was nothing gentle about the way his mouth plundered hers and she thought wildly: He's drunk! He doesn't know what he is doing. Her heart thundered tumultuously in her ears as his mouth sought the hollow of her throat, lingering in a hot exploration before venturing lower. A weakness such as she had known only once before in her life swept through her, draining her of resistance and leaving in its place the leaping flames of a desire for physical satisfaction that crowded out all reason.

In a final effort to stop him, she raised her hands to push feebly against his shoulders, but his mouth came back to hers with its undeniable demand, and her hands crawled, as if of their own free will, about his shoulders. She was vaguely aware of his hands sliding open the zipper down the skirt of her gown, then moving to unbutton the halter closing at the back of her neck. The gown slid to the floor, and Josh's hands on her skin sent shock waves through her.

A soft moan escaped her, and Josh lifted his head momentarily to look into her eyes. "Have I proved to you that you are not indifferent to me?" he asked huskily.

"Josh," she sighed protestingly as his hands explored her thrusting breasts. "Desire is not enough for a good marriage."

"Ah," he sighed, his lips moving softly against hers, "you admit that you desire me." His fingers stroked the taut tips of her breasts and he laughed deep in his throat. "But you can hardly deny it, can you?" His lips lingered tantalizingly at one corner of her mouth. "Desire may not be enough for a good marriage, but it is a wonderful place to start."

"No—"

"Yes." He laughed again, softly, and began to rid himself of his clothes, stopping frequently to kiss another vulnerable spot until, by the time he was totally undressed, her whole body was on fire with wanting him.

He pushed her gently onto the bed and followed her down until his body covered hers. Carrie groaned and squirmed beneath him. She would despise herself in the morning, she knew. But her clamoring body made it impossible for her to think about that, and as her hands moved over the hard muscles of his body she let the last restraint slip away and gave herself completely to him. It was something of a shock to her to realize that she had wanted this ever since the last time. Somewhere beyond consciousness she had yearned for such a time as this.

Chapter Eight

It was a losing of her identity. Afterward, when Carrie came back to herself, she realized that Josh was sound asleep beside her. A resentment stronger than any she had yet known took possession of her. He had taken advantage of her fragile emotional state to degrade her further, and now the alcohol he had drunk had sent him to oblivion. He probably wouldn't even remember tomorrow what had happened—but she would.

Feeling a renewed awareness of the futility of her situation, Carrie crept from the bed, put on a gown and robe, and with a blanket wrapped around her prepared to spend the remainder of the night in the big armchair in the corner of the room.

It was a long time before she could sleep, and it wasn't the cramped quarters that made slumber impossible. It was the ceaseless round of thoughts that filled her brain. What had happened with Josh was final proof of a weakness in herself that she despised. How cleverly he could manipulate her, maneuver her into getting his way. The relentless drive of his will was staggering. More than that, the hold he seemed to have over her was frightening. The stark truth was that she had never managed to overcome his will in anything important, and she had for some time doubted that she was even capable of doing so.

From the jumble of her thoughts a new idea surfaced. Was it possible that she could be falling in love with Josh? Shaken by the implications of the thought, she refused even to consider it. She could not love a man who dominated and scorned her; it would be the final humiliation.

Eventually she fell into an exhausted sleep from which she awoke repeatedly, jerking upright in her chair with a feeling of impending doom so strong that it required several moments for her to reorient herself and realize where she was. Just before dawn, upon snapping back to consciousness once more, she saw that Josh was no longer in her bed. She stumbled across the room and fell into bed, where she finally slept without waking for a few hours.

She awoke to find pale winter sunlight falling through the windows, from which draperies and undercurtains had been drawn back. In most circumstances she would have felt cheered by the clarity of the day, but her head and limbs ached. Dragging a pillow around to support her back, she sat up with a groan and held her head in her hands. Abruptly Gracie Helmstrom's high-pitched voice called to her from the hallway.

"Mrs. Revell, I've brought your breakfast up. May I come in?"

"Come." The word rasped from a throat that was too dry.

Gracie settled a tray across her knees. "It's after ten," she announced heartily. "I guess you and Mr Josh were out very late last night. Didn't seem to faze him much, though. He left the house three hours ago "

Carrie watched the girl remove a white covering cloth from an omelet, sausage links, blueberry muffins, juice, and coffee. As the smell of the food reached her nostrils, her stomach churned violently. Carrie laid her head back on the pillow and closed her eyes.

"It was Aunt Betty's idea to bring your breakfast up." There was uncertainty in Gracie's voice now. "She wanted to make it special, so she baked a batch of muffins. Nobody can make blueberry muffins like Aunt Betty."

"I'm sure the breakfast is delicious," Carrie replied, her eyes still closed. "I'm feeling a little queasy this morning. Leave the food and I'll eat what I can—and thank Betty for me."

Gracie continued to hover beside the bed. "You want some aspirin, or a doctor?"

Carrie lifted her head and opened her eyes. "No, I'll be fine."

Gracie left and Carrie poured coffee from the small pot with a hand that shook. What was wrong with her? Although she didn't know how a hangover felt, she was certain she wasn't having one now. The two glasses of wine she'd drunk at the country club could not cause such a strong reaction.

If anyone felt ill this morning, it ought to be Josh, who, according to Gracie, had gone to the office hours ago. He wasn't human, Carrie thought disconsolately, for he seemed to have none of the human frailties that plagued her.

She brought the coffee cup to her lips and sipped tentatively. When her stomach showed no sign of rejecting that, she nibbled at a muffin and took another sip of coffee. Unaccountably, she remembered how a piece of toast or a cracker had helped to settle the morning sickness that had plagued Meg during the early months of her pregnancy.

She set the coffee cup down suddenly as she realized

what she was thinking. Could she possibly be pregnant? Her body had been sidetracked from its regular cycle in recent weeks, but she had assumed that to be caused by the tense state of her nerves. She shook her head, causing the tray to jiggle. No, she couldn't be pregnant. The possibility was too remote, and she would not accept it. That did not keep her from feeling frightened, however. Another child, Josh's child, would further enmesh her in his life, trap her here without any hope of release.

Moreover, she was sure Josh would hate the idea and resent the additional obligation. He had already married her and adopted Mike; he wouldn't want a new baby by a woman whom he didn't love. Yet the sense of duty that had prompted his actions thus far would be doubly strong toward a child of his own. No, it was impossible.

Slowly she ate a portion of the large breakfast, and afterward she felt well enough to dress and go downstairs.

When Josh returned for dinner that evening, she found herself watching him for a sign that he remembered what had happened between them upon their return from the country club the night before. There was nothing, and as Carrie answered his perfunctory inquiries about Mike and listened to his abrupt replies to Ethel's questions about the dinner-dance she became convinced that he remembered little of the previous evening's events.

Miss Hastings brought Mike to them in the sitting room after dinner, and for the first time since his arrival home Josh's expression relaxed. He got down on the carpet and played with the baby, pretending to be a pony while Mike rode on his back and laughed happily. Ethel beamed at the two of them, and Carrie, from her chair in the corner, watched the spectacle with mixed feelings.

It was clear that Mike had fully accepted Josh as his father. He called him Daddy all the time now and always toddled to hug Josh's legs each time Josh appeared after being away from the house for a few hours. As for Josh, he seemed happier and more human with Mike than in any other situation.

The final adoption papers had been signed only days before, and watching man and child enjoying each other so totally, Carrie couldn't help wondering if Josh would want to divorce her soon. He had told her on the previous evening that he didn't want to discuss divorce. But, she thought bitterly, he'd had a more immediate goal in mind then, one which her stupid weakness had allowed him to accomplish.

Surely he dwelt at times on marriage to Jessica, a marriage that Carrie now believed he had been considering before he learned of Mike's existence. Would he take Mike away from her now that the baby had come to love him? Would he marry Jessica? The thought caused a bitter taste to swell in Carrie's throat. Jessica as Mike's mother? No, she would never allow that to happen. She would never give up Mike. This was the one area in which she could overcome Josh's stubborn will because she loved Mike. He was part of her life, her self, and she could not imagine living apart from him.

Josh continued to be home in time for dinner during the remaining days before Christmas, and he always spent an hour or two with Mike afterward. On the other hand, he was cold and reserved in his relationship with Carrie. Not once was there any indication in his words or manner to suggest that he remembered their lovemaking on the night of the dinner-dance.

Carrie told herself this was best, even though she was finding it more and more difficult to sleep nights. Sometimes she would toss and turn for hours, the shameful memory of Josh's lovemaking making her feel agitated and overheated and ashamed of herself for the feelings. He had mesmerized her, possessed her in some dark spiritual way. He was a devil!

In one of his rare cheerful moods, Josh spent all of Christmas day at home. Right after breakfast he took Mike into the sitting room to show the baby the array of gifts that Santa had left. Still too young to grasp the meaning of the occasion, Mike was nevertheless nearly delirious with joy over the rocking horse, the pull toys, and the wooden lawn mower that played a merry tune when it was pushed. Except for the rocking horse and some items of clothing that didn't stand a chance of catching Mike's attention with all those toys spread before him, Josh had chosen all the child's gifts.

As they exchanged presents Carrie found her depression lifting. In addition to the wallet and monogrammed silk shirts she had bought Josh a beautiful pair of silk pajamas and bedroom slippers to match. When he opened the pajamas, he looked up at her with a sardonic smile, and she felt a sudden warmth in her face. What he was thinking could not have been clearer to her if he had spoken the words aloud. Whatever had possessed her to buy him something so personal?

Ethel was warmly appreciative of the antique music box Carrie had finally found for her, and Carrie was equally delighted with the silver-handled vanity set that was Ethel's gift. After the mink she hadn't really expected anything else from Josh. But there were several gifts from him under the tree, things that, only months before, she had never even dreamed of possessing: expensive French perfume and an ivory and silver jewel case that held an emerald necklace and matching earrings. Her surprise over the extravagance of Josh's gifts allowed only a softly uttered "Thank you" to pass her lips in response.

For a few moments her spirits soared as she thought

that surely he must have some gentle feelings for her, respect at least. Then she remembered how wealthy he was, what a paltry sum the cost of her gifts must seem to him. Her depression of the past few days gradually returned.

That evening, in her bedroom, she thought back over the day—the gift exchange and the lavish dinner that had been served in the dining room at seven with Mike joining them. The little boy had been so tired and excited, however, that he ate little and was soon carried up to bed by Miss Hastings. After dinner Josh had excused himself to go to his bedroom and Ethel had pleaded weariness, retiring to her apartment.

Now Carrie sat on her bed, hearing an occasional sound from Josh's suite on the other side of the door. Unable to read, Carrie paced restlessly about the room, remembering the gifts Josh had given her and the brief thanks she had managed in return. She really had not shown much gratitude, and she decided she must before she would be able to sleep.

Taking a deep breath, she walked to the connecting door and knocked.

Josh's voice bidding her enter sounded gruff and distracted. He was sitting at his desk, a pile of papers scattered over the top. He was wearing his toast velour robe and the pajamas and bedroom slippers she had given him. He lifted his head, running a hand through his hair.

"I'm sorry. I'm interrupting your work, aren't I?" Carrie said.

"Yes, but it's all right." He turned more toward her, dropping on the desk the pen he was holding. "What do you want?"

"I—I didn't thank you properly for your gifts."

He lifted his shoulders as though the matter were of little concern to him. "I'm glad you're pleased." Then, with a slight smile: "I believe I once told you that you might adjust to being a Revell."

She frowned. "If you are suggesting that I want to stay married to you for material advantage, you're wrong."

"Oh?" His tone was mocking. "Then you have another reason?"

"Reason for what?" He was confusing her, and, twisting her fingers together, she walked to a window and looked out at the darkness.

"For wanting to stay married to me," he told her, with scorn lacing the words.

She turned to face him. "I don't—I mean—" She halted abruptly, discovering that she felt hot and increasingly nervous. It seemed necessary to say something, however, so she blurted out, "I'm glad the pajamas fit."

He glanced at the silk-clad legs that were now stretched out before him. "Perfectly. I decided to use them for lounging, since, as you must know, I sleep in the raw."

"Yes," she replied with rising confusion. "I can't imagine what made me buy them. It's difficult to know what to give you."

His head tilted to one side as he gazed at her. "I shouldn't think that would be difficult at all."

"I've been thinking," she went on, unwilling to try to unravel his meaning; "I would like to know more about the family business. I was wondering if you would be willing to take me around, show me the operation."

He continued to gaze at her with a mocking lift at the corners of his mouth. "Has Kevin turned you down?"

"No!" His relaxed slouch in the chair irritated her beyond all reason. How dare he be relaxed while she felt tied in knots! "I haven't asked him."

"I hope that is the truth, Carrie. I meant what I said

about your not spending time alone with him. I won't have my wife carrying on an affair with another man."

"If I told you I have no personal interest in Kevin, you wouldn't believe me, would you?"

"I would find it difficult to swallow. I'm in a position to know that under that uptight exterior there is a deep sensuality. Once a woman like you has been . . . awakened, it is hard for her to live without love."

For a moment Carrie could not find the words to express her outrage.

"Tell me, Carrie, isn't that why you are really here?" He thrust his hands into his robe pockets, and the muscles in his long legs stood out clearly beneath the silk of his pajamas.

"I came in here to thank you for your gifts—nothing more."

"You're a poor liar, my dear," he said, his voice hard.

If only he would not look at her with such contempt! Somewhere in the confusion of her overheated motives there was a desire to be taken in his arms, to feel them around her, to feel his body touching hers. But not with scorn mixed with it.

Against her will, some of the hurt she was feeling softened her voice. "The only times you have touched me have been with naked lust, or when you were in a drunken stupor." Somehow she managed to push down the memory of the moments of tenderness, the amazing glimpses of gentleness she had seen in him when he was fully aroused. She rushed on. "You have never been convinced that I am not, at heart, a promiscuous, conniving woman, have you? Even though you know I was a virgin when I married you. I just can't understand—"

Her words seemed finally to have disturbed his arrogant indifference. He straightened in his chair, and before she realized what he meant to do, he had reached out and, grasping her arm, jerked her onto his lap. She squirmed in the cramped position, but he held her against him with cruel hands.

"Are you the sort of woman who can only enjoy sex when it is forced upon her?"

She felt the hardness of his body beneath her as, with one hand, he forced her chin around so that his mouth could settle on hers, parting her lips and possessing them with a harshness that gave her physical pain. When at last he released her chin and lifted his head, his eyes scanned her features with unrelenting ruthlessness.

"Don't look so surprised." He moved, allowing his arms to drop away from her at last. "Isn't that what you came in here for? Perhaps you are now having second thoughts. What a vacillating creature you are! But don't worry—I won't take advantage of your weakness and carry you to bed."

His words and icy gaze hurt her more than she had thought possible. She covered her face with her hands and cried, "You are mean and selfish and crude. There is not one spark of human feeling in you!"

Hearing his breathing become labored, she snatched her hands away and saw deep anger darkening his face. Fear stiffened her as he gripped her arms so roughly that a cry was wrenched from her. She thought he would fling her aside or shake her, but he seemed to gain control of himself and pushed her from his lap, allowing her to gain her balance and stand.

"Don't," he said warningly, "decide to throw the emeralds back at me as you did the mink. I won't put up with any more tantrums, Carrie."

Crushed by the bitterness in the words, she did not even have the strength to argue. The anger drained out of her as she stared down at him, feeling a resurgence of the nausea that had been plaguing her in the mornings.

In that moment she knew with a cold certainty that overcame all her unwillingness and rationalizations that she was carrying Josh's child. This man who looked at her with such contempt had made her pregnant, and now he taunted her with her weakness in giving in to him.

She hugged herself to stop the shaking. "Good night, Josh."

She had reached the door before he spoke in a tone that was devoid of expression. "When you are willing to be honest about your feelings, Carrie, come back."

The door closed with a sharp click behind her.

Before going down for breakfast the next morning, Carrie dressed in an old shirt and jeans. She had not slept well, and her heart was heavy. In fact, she felt about as faded as her clothing. Not that it mattered how she dressed; Josh had made it plain that his attitude toward her would remain indifferent, no matter what she wore.

It was almost eight when she entered the dining room, and she was surprised to see Josh just starting breakfast. She had no desire to face him in her present mood, but she had little choice after he looked up and saw her.

"Good morning, Carrie."

He said it as if he were amused by the hesitancy in her manner. This thought made her rebellious. He might feel no tenderness for her, but he had married her and this was her home for as long as she remained here. She would not be made to seem an outsider in her own house!

As she sat down Josh went on. "I hope you slept well."

"Quite well, thank you." They were silent as Betty came in to serve Carrie.

When the housekeeper left, Josh's eyes raked over

Carrie with an intolerant expression. "I must say you look rather drawn for someone who has had a good night's rest."

"I haven't put on any makeup yet," said Carrie defensively.

"It seems the honeymoon is over," said Josh with heavy sarcasm.

His taunting attitude infuriated her. She lifted her eyes and glared at him. "Honeymoon? Is that what you call these last weeks? Strange, but I would call them something much less romantic than that!"

His eyes narrowed as he lifted a napkin to his mouth slowly. In his navy suit and white shirt he looked devastatingly attractive. Carrie had a quickly stifled impulse to apologize for what she had just said and to try to take a first step toward a more amiable relationship with him. But the sneer that twisted his lips as the napkin came away stopped her.

"Are you complaining about the lack of romance in your life? If you are longing for romance, Carrie, it can't be with your husband since you find me so distasteful that, after your flesh is satisfied, you prefer sleeping in a chair to sharing a bed with me."

"It wasn't—I'm not—" She stopped, furious at the way he always managed to confuse her. How like him to hide his memory of that night following the dinner-dance until he could use it against her. She was sick of being put on the defensive! "Fortunately, you aren't inconvenienced by my attitude. I'm sure Jessica is more than willing to take care of your—needs."

"Your jealous suspicions are beginning to wear a little thin," he replied levelly. "But since you've brought up Jessica's name—"

"I just wish we would never have to see her again," Carrie interrupted involuntarily.

His eyes glittered. "I have no intention of being made to look the fool by my wife's refusal to see an old friend. Do you really think I would insult her because of some whim of yours?" he inquired in a voice that was too calm.

Carrie forced herself to meet his steely gaze, in spite of the erratic staccato of her heart. "No," she snapped, her eyes wide with anger. "You receive too many benefits from that 'old friendship' to insult Jessica, don't you?"

With an abrupt, impatient movement, he shoved back his chair and stood. "If you want to fight with me, Carrie," he grated, "do it somewhere else besides the dining room where one of the servants or my mother might overhear us. We will say no more about Jessica." He turned and left the room, going toward the back hall and the garage.

In an unconscious gesture, Carrie twisted her wedding ring nervously round and round. I'll take some of that arrogance out of him, she vowed, and I won't take any further insults from his mistress.

Chapter Nine

Early in January Josh spent three days in Washington on business. He did not ask Carrie to accompany him, and she was both relieved and resentful of his continuing indifference. The day after his return, they celebrated Mike's first birthday with cake, ice cream, and more gifts. Josh was surprisingly indulgent; he even got out his camera and snapped pictures during the family celebration. But he could also be firm, and his manner with Mike told Carrie that as the boy grew older Josh would apply discipline as well as love. As a husband he was impossible, but he was, Carrie admitted grudgingly, a very good father.

One morning later in the month, Josh surprised her by coming into her bedroom before leaving for work and announcing, "Today would be a good day to show you around the plant, if you care to come down later on."

It was the first mention he had made of introducing her to the family business since she had expressed an interest weeks before. Contrary to her conviction, he had not dismissed the idea or forgotten it. "Would ten be all right?"

"Fine. I'll see you then." He left her, and she looked at the closed door with some bewilderment. Would she ever be able to guess what was going on behind his stony face? Shrugging, she settled more comfortably against her pillow and sipped the coffee Gracie had brought up with her breakfast a few minutes earlier. Betty and her niece seemed bent on pampering Carrie, and she was finding that she rather enjoyed a long, leisurely breakfast in bed. In fact, she drew it out as long as possible, for it helped to fill some time in days that were often lonely. She found that she was looking forward to going to the plant.

Later she dressed warmly in raspberry colored wool slacks and a gray-and-raspberry-striped turtleneck sweater. She wore black leather boots for protection in the deep snow and her heavy white wool coat with a black and white knitted scarf wound snugly around her neck.

As she drove the Corvette into town she felt good to be going somewhere with a purpose. Turning through the gates into the Revell Corporation's grounds, she was waved ahead by a guard who apparently recognized her. Evidently Josh had left word of her expected arrival.

Josh's offices were in the largest of the buff-brick office buildings in the southeast corner of the grounds. Carrie entered a large reception area furnished with several leather couches and a walnut desk behind which sat an attractive young woman who looked up and smiled at Carrie.

"I'm Mrs. Revell. My husband is expecting me."

The young woman got up and came around the desk, her smile bright. "I'm so happy to meet you. I'm Mr.

Revell's secretary, Charlotte Minson. He wanted to be informed the minute you arrived. If you would like to sit down, I'll go and tell him." After they shook hands, she disappeared through a door leading to a carpeted hallway.

She was back momentarily, followed by Josh. "Come to my office for a minute, Carrie." Carrie felt the secretary's eyes on them as she preceded Josh down the hall. He directed her into an office at the end.

It was similar to Kevin Hamilton's office, paneled walls and shag carpeting, but larger and with an adjoining kitchenette that contained a bar, refrigerator, countertop range, microwave oven, and a table with four chairs. "I usually have lunch here," Josh explained. "It's faster and more convenient."

"Does Charlotte cook for you?" Carrie inquired.

He laughed. "Charlotte is too liberated for that. I wouldn't risk losing a good secretary by asking her. I fend for myself, although I confess I stock up at the delicatessen frequently."

Carrie was surprised. "What are you having today?"

"Chicken salad, relishes, and toasted French bread. The *pièce de résistance* is cheesecake from the local bakery. I was hoping you would join me."

He apparently intended to spend several hours showing her around, and Carrie was bewildered by his willingness to take so much time from his demanding work. Whatever had brought about this new considerate attitude, she much preferred it to the open antagonism that usually characterized their times together. "That sounds very nice."

She had been examining the microwave oven, and when she turned back to him, he was contemplating her with a musing look. He said briskly, "We're going to see the sawmill first. Ready?"

It took more than three hours to tour the sawmill and

the paper mill with Josh. Not surprisingly, he was an extremely knowledgeable and informative guide. What was surprising to Carrie was the patience with which he encouraged her to ask about anything she didn't understand and then provided illuminating replies. In this situation, separate from their personal lives, he seemed almost a different man. She felt more on equal terms with him than at any time since their marriage.

After their return to his office, Josh insisted that she allow him to prepare their lunch. It amounted to nothing more than popping the food into the micro-wave oven and placing paper plates and cups on the table, but Carrie found the total lack of self-consciousness with which he moved about the small kitchenette disconcerting. Heretofore she had pictured him as always giving orders and being waited upon.

The food was good, too, and the cheesecake was as mouthwatering as he had led her to believe. It was the most relaxed time they had ever spent together, and Carrie lingered over the meal, reluctant to have it end.

"It's considerate of you to take so much time away from your work," she said at one point, "just to satisfy my curiosity."

"I've enjoyed it," he said, looking as if he were slightly surprised by the admission. "It's gratifying that my wife is so interested in what I do. To tell you the truth, I thought you might be only pretending interest."

"For what reason?" Carrie asked with astonishment.

He lifted his shoulders and smiled slightly. "In the interest of some devious female ruse, I suppose."

Carrie felt herself bridling. "Do you still feel that way?"

He shook his head. "It's been obvious all morning that your interest is genuine."

Seeing the meditative look in his eyes, Carrie asked, "Why is that so hard for you to believe?"

"I haven't known many women who cared for much beyond their creature comforts," he replied tersely.

"Ethel told me once," Carrie ventured, "that your first wife wasn't interested in the family business."

Although his position in the chair did not visibly shift, she sensed a sudden tensing of his muscles. "What else did Mother tell you about Helen?"

Confused by the alertness she now saw in him, Carrie faltered. "Only that she died in Toronto and that she was carrying your child."

Disappointment clamped over Carrie's heart as she saw the closed look returning to his face. "Mother has no business discussing my past with you." He pushed back his chair and, picking up the used paper plates and cups, walked to the trash can and tossed them in. He stood with his back to her, hands thrust into his trousers pockets.

"I'm sure she meant no harm, Josh," Carrie said, wishing that she had not mentioned Helen. "She loves you very much, and she's extremely proud of you. She—she was trying to help me understand you a little better."

He turned then and eyed her carefully. "I didn't know you were interested in understanding me." He ran a hand through his tawny hair. "I'm sorry. You're right. Mother's intentions are always good. It's just that her outlook has been influenced by the protected life she has led."

Carrie frowned. "I don't understand. If you mean that Ethel is basically optimistic, then that's true, but—"

"It doesn't matter," Josh interrupted. "I'd prefer not to discuss Helen with you, if you don't mind."

His curt manner made Carrie feel like an outcast. "Of course. Thank you for lunch. I'd better go now. Mike likes me to put him down for his nap."

He gave her a long, brooding look, and she thought

for a moment that he might be going to ask her to stay a
bit longer. But before he could speak there was a knock
at the outer office door and Kevin Hamilton's voice
reached them. "Josh, your secretary's gone to lunch, so
I'm barging in."

Josh walked into the adjoining office. "Come in,
Kevin. We've just finished lunch."

Kevin advanced into the room and saw Carrie
standing in the kitchenette doorway. "Oh, hi, Carrie. I
didn't know you were here. I wouldn't have interrupted
if I had."

"I was about to leave, anyway," Carrie told him. She
walked to the small closet and took out her coat which
Josh had hung there earlier.

Kevin glanced from Carrie to Josh, clearly uncomfortable about walking in on them. "Josh, I have to go
into town and pick up some papers from the attorney,
but I left my car in the shop today."

Carrie, who had been occupied with buttoning her
coat, spoke without thinking. "I'm going right through
town. You can ride with me and then I can drive you
back."

"That's too much of an imposition," Kevin said. "I
thought I might borrow Josh's car."

Carrie felt Josh's gaze upon her and looked up to
meet eyes that were glazed with ice. "I'm sure Carrie
would enjoy chauffeuring you, Kevin."

"Well, uh . . ." Clearly Kevin did not know what to
say. "If you're sure . . ."

Carrie was tempted to say there was something
she must do in town that she had until now forgotten
and that she wouldn't be able to take Kevin after all.
But Josh's rigidly angry stance and the way his face had
hardened into a scornful mask changed her mind.
He was being totally unreasonable in his attitude
toward her friendship with Kevin. It must be his own

guilty conscience that was bothering him, Carrie thought, her resolve stiffening. Undoubtedly he expected her to behave with the same deceit that he and Jessica employed.

"It's no trouble at all, Kevin," she said, dragging her gaze from Josh's tense face. "Goodbye, Josh."

When she got back to the house after returning Kevin to the plant, she found that Miss Hastings had already put Mike to bed. Unwilling to retire to her bedroom, where there was nothing to do but brood over Josh's infuriating shifts in mood, she went in to chat with Ethel.

The older woman ordered tea for both of them, then settled back on the chaise longue with her knitting to inquire about Carrie's visit to the plant.

"It was fascinating," Carrie told her truthfully. "I was impressed by the size of the operation. I want to know more about everything, even those copper mines in South Africa." She paused, seeing a wince of pain drift across Ethel's face. "I'm sorry, Mother. I must have reminded you of Danny."

"It's all right," Ethel assured her. "It's natural that you should be interested in the mines. You must ask Josh to take you to South Africa with him the next time he goes."

"I'd probably only be in the way," Carrie evaded.

Ethel's blue eyes widened. "Of course you wouldn't be. I'm sure Josh would be happy to have you accompany him. It's wonderful that you want to go." As usual, Ethel was jumping to optimistic conclusions, but Carrie didn't have the heart to disillusion her. If her marriage were a normal one, she would love traveling to South Africa with her husband. As it was, being forced to live in such close proximity for weeks would only cause more tension between her and Josh.

Remembering Josh's extreme reaction to her mention of his first wife, Carrie now said, "Helen wasn't interested in the family business, was she? I confess I'm a little curious about her. What was she like?"

"Oh, my dear, that is difficult to say. She was a lovely girl, took a lot of pride in her appearance. She and Josh were a striking couple, both tall and blond. And she was so vital, always on the go. But at times I thought I glimpsed another side to Helen. Wasn't it Twain who said that everybody has a dark side that he never shows to other people? Well, a few times I sensed that in Helen." She blinked and laughed a little uneasily, as if she realized she was saying too much about Josh's first wife. "Josh's father always told me I was too fanciful. I expect he was right." She sat straighter. "I am sure that Helen was the vibrant, lovely woman she appeared to be. Actually, her only real fault—I'm not even sure you could call it a fault—was her refusal to take an interest in Josh's affairs." She frowned slightly. "It made it difficult for him to talk to her about what he did all day, you see. As for you, you want to know about all the areas of Josh's life, and that is as it should be. Married couples should have interests in common, and already there is more of that between you and Josh than there was for him with Helen. You're going to learn about the business, and, of course, there is Mike .   "

All during this rambling discourse, Carrie had felt a protest rising to her lips. She was continually amazed by Ethel's determination to see Josh's marriage in romantic terms. It was true that Carrie was interested in the business and that she shared Josh's devotion to Mike. As for there being more between her and Josh than there had been in Josh's first marriage, that was laughable. He had loved Helen, and his lack of love for Carrie had created a gulf between them that seemed to grow wider with time. It was laughable, only she felt

like anything but laughing. In fact, she had to blink
rapidly to combat the moisture that was blurring her
vision.

"Why, Carrie, dear, what is it? I've upset you by
running on about Helen, haven't I?"

"No." Carrie brushed at her eyes with one hand and
excused herself. "I believe I'll go up and rest for an
hour or so."

"Your visit to the plant must have been too much for
you," Ethel said.

Carrie murmured a vague assent and went upstairs,
where, instead of lying down, she paced restlessly like a
caged cat. The lessening of strain that she had experienced that morning had completely dissipated and now
she felt more tense than ever. She refused dinner when
Gracie came up to tell her it was ready and instead
cleaned out and rearranged her closet and bureau
drawers. She had to keep busy or she would fly apart at
the seams. This activity filled the time until after nine,
when she decided to seek relaxation in a hot bubble
bath, where she languished for the better part of an
hour.

She was sitting at her dressing table in gown and
robe, filing her fingernails, when Josh knocked at her
door and, without waiting for an answer, walked in.
"Mother says you're not feeling well."

Glancing up at his tall frame standing, legs slightly
apart, in the middle of the room as if he had come to do
battle, Carrie retorted, "Your husbandly concern over-
whelms me."

"Well, it seems our relationship is back to normal,"
he commented. "You shouldn't try to schedule your
husband and your boyfriend on the same day. Leading
a double life is apparently too much of a strain on you."

Carrie realized that she was clutching the nail file so
hard that it was digging into her palm. She relaxed her

grip and put the file aside. "I will have to take lessons from you so I will know how to handle it," she snapped.

His brown eyes glinted. "Does he commiserate with you over what a poor misunderstood wife you are? Does he comfort you?"

"You're totally irrational on the subject of Kevin, and you know it. There is nothing but casual friendship between us. I'm a married woman."

"You aren't going to tell me that that makes any difference to Kevin Hamilton! Fortunately, you seem to be more cautious. You brought him back to the plant promptly this afternoon."

"You timed us, I presume."

"Yes," he said unabashedly.

Carrie felt outraged. "Next I suppose you will have me followed."

"I hope it doesn't come to that, Carrie."

She felt at a disadvantage, sitting there while he glared down at her from his towering height. She walked stiffly to a window and turned to face him. "Checking up on me is not necessary, nor will it ever be as long as we are together. Is it too much to ask that you at least trust me that far?"

"I have found little reason to trust women," he responded coolly.

She swung away to hide the slight tremble of her lips and heard him approaching her. He lifted her hair and brushed the back of her neck with warm fingers. "That doesn't mean I can't appreciate their other attributes." Carrie knew by the sound of his voice that he was smiling.

She turned swiftly, rubbing her neck as if to rid it of the glow his touch had left. "You expect me to settle for that? You have the arrogance to believe that I am just waiting to fall into your arms the moment you touch me! Josh Revell, you are conceited, self-centered, and—" She floundered, searching for something that would hurt him as deeply as he had hurt her. "And your touch makes my skin crawl!"

His lips tightened into a thin line. He walked to the door of his suite and slammed it behind him.

She could not even imagine sleeping after that. She didn't go to bed but sat in a chair, forcing her eyes to scan the lines of a mystery novel she had found downstairs in the study. She was barely able to follow the story and kept running across names of characters whom she could not remember, much less place in the flow of events. Well after midnight, she tossed the book aside.

It was no longer possible to avoid thinking about Josh. He was cruel and infuriating, but she had had her part in their worsening relationship. Something in him put her instantly on the defensive, and she was always too quick to return taunt for taunt, abuse for abuse. Divorce was inevitable if things continued on their present course, but she admitted to herself for the first time that she didn't really want that. Not only would she run the risk of losing Mike, but in less than seven months she would be responsible for another child. She knew that if anyone was to divert the collision course along which she and Josh were rushing, it would have to be she; she would have to make the overtures. Somehow just admitting this made her feel a little calmer.

So far she had discovered only one way to communicate with Josh. Before she had time to examine her doubts, she went to the connecting door and, opening it softly, stepped into Josh's bedroom. Faint light from the yard lamps outside revealed his long form stretched full length under the covers. He lay on his back, one arm flung above his head across the pillow. She stared down at him for only a moment, and as she watched, his eyes opened. In the shadowy dimness it was impossible to discern at exactly what instant this had happened, and she started when she realized that he was looking back at her.

"Are you awake?"

"Yes." His whisper sounded as insubstantial as the shadows.

Carrie took a step that brought her next to the bed. Now she could see the bareness of his shoulders above the covers, the hard muscles in his arms. "I came to apologize." There was no response, only that unwavering look. "When you make me angry, I say things that I don't really mean."

"Don't you?" There was no inflection in the words. He did not believe her, or if he did he didn't care.

"Please, Josh." She pushed down a sob. "I don't want to live in an armed camp. At the office this morning I felt we were moving closer to each other. I shouldn't have offered to drive Kevin, knowing how you felt. I'm sorry."

He did not move. "I see. It's forgotten, then. I won't mention it again."

But there was no kindness in his voice. Couldn't he sense that she was miserable, that she needed love and reassurance? But she had only asked to be forgiven for her actions that morning, and perhaps he really believed that was all she wanted.

"I—I haven't slept at all. Have you?"

"No," he admitted.

"I'm lonely." She had started to shiver, standing there beside the bed.

His eyes moved at last and ran over her, but she sensed that there was no softening in their shadowy depths. If she were Jessica Thorpe, would he continue to regard her with such detachment? She had an impulse to retreat, return to the chair in her room to wait out the night. But stubborn defiance surged through her. She was his wife. She had the right to be there! Bending, she lifted the covers and slid into his bed. "I'm cold," she said.

Now that she was there, she was suddenly amazed at her brazenness and lay stiffly, not touching him. If he told her to leave now, she would die of humiliation. Tears formed and slowly ran down her cheeks. Surreptitiously she wiped her eyes with a corner of the sheet.

He moved then, turning on his side and wrapping his arms around her shivering body, pulling her against him, where she began to relax in the warmth of his body. His nakedness shocked her momentarily, but she pulled her mind away from it and, sighing, curled closer to him. He raised himself on one elbow and looked down at her.

As if of its own will, her hand went up to touch his cheek and the cleft in his chin. "Josh," she whispered.

He caught her hand and brought it to his lips, kissing the palm with a slow gentleness. "Do you know what you are asking for?"

She nodded.

"And it's what you want?"

Again she nodded.

"Then," he said, sighing raggedly, "let's get rid of all these clothes."

A moment later she was snuggled against him, her body radiating pleasure all along its length as it touched his. His hand fondled her breast and his lips found the secret places of her body, bringing her quickly to flaming arousal. His body pressed against hers and their lips met, and her arms clung to him fiercely, holding him to her. Oh, this was what she had wanted, to give her body to him with unrestrained love—and more than her body, her heart and soul, herself.

His lips trailed down her neck and across her shoulders. "Your body is more beautiful to me every time I see it."

"Josh," she whispered, wanting to break down all the barriers between them, to put her love into words. But he was breathing heavily and kissing her with heightened urgency.

"I adore your body, Carrie," he groaned and she heard the words in a daze as her pleasure mounted to meet his and culminated with explosive intensity.

When it was over, she lay still in his arms. She felt the golden glow fading, and she didn't want to let it go. She wanted to tell him everything, even about the baby. "Josh?"

There was no answer. He was asleep, already separated from her. Feeling utterly bereft, she stared into the shadows for long minutes, remembering the closeness she had felt while he made love to her, remembering the other times. "I adore your body," he had said in the throes of his passion. But that was so very different from loving *her*. Never once, not even when desire drove him, had he said that he loved her. Whatever Josh Revell was, he was not a deceiver.

She moved from beneath his arm, and he did not stir. She slipped out of bed, picked up her discarded night clothes, and returned to her own bedroom. Unable to make head or tail of her gown in the darkness, she turned on the dressing-table lamp and caught a glimpse of herself in the mirror. Dropping the gown, she stared at her naked body, still tender with the afterglow of lovemaking. Her stomach was still flat, but her breasts were already noticeably fuller. In a month or two she would not be able to hide her pregnancy from Josh. Her body was the only thing that drew him, but when she lost her figure would he even want to look at her? Would he find her ugly and repulsive?

One hand came up to her mouth to stifle a groan of misery. She was helplessly in love with him. There was no hope of changing that now. She had never been in love before, and she knew herself well enough to realize that she would probably never love anyone but Josh, no matter how he hurt her. How often she had heard that trite expression, a one-man woman, and had laughed. Well, trite or not, it seemed that she was such a woman.

Chapter Ten

The next morning Josh came into her bedroom before going to work. "I missed you when I awoke to find you gone. I was hoping for a return engagement."

Why did he say it like that? As if their lovemaking were no more important than a business meeting for which an appointment had to be made. "You fell asleep and I—I saw no reason to stay."

"You didn't?" He looked at her, sitting propped up in bed with the covers tucked about her body, and shook his head. "Don't tell me I hurt your feelings by falling asleep!" A devilish twinkle came into his eyes. "Didn't I satisfy you, Carrie?"

She was blushing, and he was enjoying it! "Yes—I mean, no—"

"No?" His eyebrows rose in amused disbelief.

"I am more than a body," she said. "I wanted to talk."

"Talk!" He laughed, and some of the masculine

condescension she had come to know so well touched his features. "Why do women always want to talk everything to death? We seem to communicate very well. Why spoil it with tedious analyses?"

Spoil it! Didn't he realize that it was his insensitive attitude that spoiled it for her? She turned her face away from him. "You will never understand me."

He gripped her chin and forced her to look at him. All the amusement was gone from his eyes. "What more do you want from me, Carrie? I've given you things you never had—"

"Things!" she cried.

His fingers gripped tighter, immobilizing her head. "You are like all women. You want to unman me. You want to pry into all the secrets of my soul so that you will have ammunition against me when you want to manipulate me." His eyes blazed into hers. "Well, forget it, Carrie. I never make the same mistake twice." He let her go suddenly, and she shrank back against the pillow away from his anger.

He didn't want a real marriage. She was nothing more than a kept woman to him. "All right, Josh," she said huskily. "I see that I've been stupidly naïve to expect any human impulses from a—a sex machine. Last night, and the other times, too, resulted from weakness on my part. I may make the same mistake twice, but I don't repeat it indefinitely."

"Is that a threat?" Every inch of his long, lean body was stiff with outrage.

"Yes," she returned.

The hands hanging at his sides clenched, and she knew that his first instinct was to cause her physical pain. She was so angry and humiliated herself that she almost wished he would hit her so that she would have an excuse to claw his taut face. But after a brief moment he had himself under rigid control. "When it comes to a battle of wills, Carrie, you are out of your league!" He spun on his heel and strode out, slamming the door behind him.

The blood left Carrie's face and she felt light-headed and nauseated. She pressed one hand against her stomach where his child was growing, and her breakfast rose in her throat. She swallowed convulsively, lying without moving until the nausea subsided.

She had been incredibly foolish to imagine that going to him last night would change anything. What insanity had prompted her to do it? But she knew the answer to that. Her mind might rebel, but her body craved his touch. Some primitive need in her built and built, fraying her nerves and keeping her awake nights, until every fiber and cell cried out for the assuagement that only he could give. It was just that simple—and that frightening. He had created this sensual need and because of it he had gained a tremendous hold on her. The baby she was carrying would give him another hold. Slowly she was becoming his prisoner.

Her thoughts were creating such anxiety in her that she couldn't keep still. She got out of bed and dressed hurriedly, going along the hallway to the nursery. Miss Hastings would have a free morning. Carrie would bathe Mike, give him his breakfast, and play with him in order to keep her mind occupied with something besides Josh; otherwise, her nerves would soon be stretched to the breaking point.

That morning was the beginning of a cold war between her and Josh. If she had thought him cool and aloof before, she soon learned that their former clashes had amounted to mere skirmishes. This was worse, this total indifference which amounted to a virtual refusal to acknowledge her existence. Even when they were in the same room together, she felt as if he were miles away.

February brought more snow and freezing temperatures, and as the third month of Carrie's pregnancy progressed she was shut in the house with Mike, Ethel, and the servants for days on end, and every single day seemed to drag on interminably. One of the rare occasions during that time when Josh took any notice of her was when she mentioned to Ethel over dinner one evening that she thought she would drive into town the next day.

"You can't drive on these roads," he had said in a tone that brooked no argument. "It's too dangerous."

She had been unable to stop some of her bitterness from spilling out. "It *would* be a shame to damage the car."

He had fixed her with a stabbing look. "You sound like a sulky child. You'll have to occupy yourself here, and that's all there is to it."

Then he had left the table, and Ethel had glanced at Carrie with a bewildered look. "I've rarely seen Josh so unapproachable. Something is very wrong, Carrie. Would it help to talk about it?"

Carrie sagged in her chair, feeling as if her body were made of lead. "No," she said disconsolately. She made an effort to perk up for Ethel's sake. "It's just that being unable to get out of the house for so long is making me nervous. Don't worry about Josh and me, Mother. We'll work things out."

Her attempt at reassurance sounded false in her own ears. Far from imagining that they would work things out, she was coming, more and more, to accept the inevitable conclusion that she and Josh could not stay together. They would destroy each other.

During the week following that confrontation, she hardly saw Josh at all. He left the house before she awoke and worked until very late every evening. Ethel told Carrie that Josh was working against a deadline for some large deliveries of both lumber and paper. In what Carrie knew was an attempt to comfort her, Ethel added that the delays in production that were causing the problem didn't happen often. She was sure the situation would improve in a few days.

One afternoon she was having tea with Ethel in her apartment when Betty appeared to announce Jessica Thorpe. Jessica, wrapped in fur from chin to midcalf and wearing fur-lined boots, swept in, snow frosting her black hair. Her exuberant spirits seemed foreign in the quiet house.

"I had to come and see how the shut-ins were doing," she caroled as she shrugged off her coat and settled into a chair.

"We're acquiring prison pallor," Ethel returned with a laugh, "but otherwise we're coping. Jessie, what possessed you to come out here in this weather?"

"Guilt," Jessica said. "I've neglected you too long." She reached out to pat Ethel's shoulder. "Josh keeps telling me you're all right, but I wanted to see for myself."

"You are so thoughtful," Ethel told her, "but you're taking an unnecessary risk, driving over five miles of snow-packed road."

"I have snow tires," Jessica said dismissively, "and I drove very carefully."

Ethel smiled at her, then lifted the teapot which sat on the table beside her, pouring some of the steaming liquid into a cup. "This will warm your insides." She handed the cup to Jessica. "I confess we are delighted to have a visitor, especially one who is in such high spirits. Aren't we, Carrie?"

Carrie, who had been sipping her tea and watching Jessica over the cup's rim, murmured, "Yes. Ethel and I have about exhausted each other's store of interesting conversational topics." She was wondering when Josh had found time to keep Jessica apprised of Ethel's welfare. As usual, she imagined the worst, but she told herself it would have required only a brief phone call. She suspected that Jessica's avowed concern for Ethel gave the woman an excuse to phone Josh frequently.

"Then I'll bring you up on all the latest gossip in town. But first, where is your little boy? Josh tells me he's beginning to say a few words."

Jessica's repeated references to Josh seemed intentional, and Carrie tried not to display any reaction. "He's napping."

"Well," said Jessica, settling more comfortably into her chair with her teacup in both hands, "I am prepared to stay until he wakes up. Our second meeting has been delayed far too long."

Sensing an implied criticism, Carrie said, "The weather has been too bad to take him out."

"You're a very conscientious mother, Carrie," Jessica said and then turned to Ethel. "Has Josh gotten those problems ironed out at the paper mill? He was telling me last night that— No, I spoke to him on the phone last night. It was the night before last when he came by the house. Anyway, the minute I saw him I knew something was wrong. He said a dozen employees have been out with the flu and two of the machines were out of order."

Carrie realized that she was clutching an empty cup and abruptly set it down. Then she twisted her hands together in her lap as the implication in Jessica's rambling monologue hit her. Josh had been with Jessica at her house two nights ago when he had said he was working late.

"I know they got the machines running again," Ethel was saying, seeming oblivious to the clear evidence that Josh was carrying on an affair with Jessica.

Carrie got to her feet and Ethel stopped what she was saying to glance at her. "Do you want more tea, dear?"

"No. I think I'd better go check on Mike." She started for the door.

"Don't forget I want to see him," Jessica called after her.

Carrie stopped with her hand on the knob but did not look back. "If you're still here when he wakes up, I'll have Miss Hastings bring him down."

She didn't go to the nursery but to her bedroom, where she was still sitting in the armchair, an afghan over her legs, trying not to think about Josh and Jessica together, when Ethel tapped at the door and called her name.

It was the first time her mother-in-law had ever come to her room, and Carrie hurried to open the door. "What is it, Mother? Are you ill?"

"Gracious, no. I was worried about you."

When they were seated, Ethel went on, "It's growing dark already. Jessie waited as long as she dared, but she finally said she would have to see Mike another time. She didn't want to drive after dark." When Carrie did not respond, Ethel's tone became sympathetic. "Jessie upset you, didn't she? You looked so—well, crushed, when you left."

"That shouldn't surprise you," Carrie said, unable for once to hide her resentment from her mother-in-law.

"Carrie," said Ethel seriously, "I know it was what she said about Josh being at her house recently. My dear, you're making too much of it. They've known each other for years. I'm sure there is an innocent explanation. Josh could have married Jessica if he had wanted, but he married you." How simple it was for Ethel with her rose-colored glasses.

"I wish I could be as optimistic as you are," Carrie said, meaning it.

"You must ask Josh why he went to Jessie's when he comes home. Don't let these little misunderstandings fester."

Little misunderstandings! Carrie felt an impulse toward hysterical laughter at the understatement. Looking into Ethel's pale, gentle face, however, she couldn't bring herself to give voice to the recriminations against Josh that were flying around in her brain. Instead, she managed a weak smile. "Thank you for always being kind and understanding. You have made me feel so welcome since I came here."

"Carrie, this is your home because it is Josh's."

"I know," said Carrie, "but it's sweet of you to say it, anyway."

When Ethel left her, Carrie stared out a window into the late-afternoon gloom. She felt a nerve jumping in her temple and another jerking along her arm. She had to get away, if only for a little while, in order to admit to herself what a part of her had known for a long time. She and Josh could not stay together. She had to leave him and get a divorce, and she had to take Mike with her. She did not know how to accomplish this or when, except that it would have to be soon. Perhaps if she were separated from him she could begin to get over him. But even as she sat thinking this, she knew it was a futile hope. The child she was carrying would be a constant reminder of him.

She stripped down to her slip and got into bed, lying on her back with the covers pulled up to her chin. She stared unseeing at the ceiling for a long time before she napped, wondering how she would manage to leave with Mike without anyone's knowing until it was too late to stop her.

Chapter Eleven

In the event, it proved to be easier than she could have imagined. An uncommonly bright winter sun shone for the next two days, melting some of the snow, and the snowplows finally cleared the road leading from town past the Revell estate. On the morning of the third day, Carrie was having her breakfast in the kitchen when Adam mentioned to Betty that he was going to town to pick up some yard tools. It was the opportunity Carrie had been waiting for.

"Adam," she said, "would you mind if Mike and I rode into town with you? I'd like to spend the day with Julia Freemont."

"It will be good for you to go," Betty commented.

"Oh, yes," Carrie assured her, "and I've been promising Julia to bring Mike in to see her."

"Can you be ready to go by ten?" Adam wanted to know. Carrie said that she could and after breakfast went back up to her bedroom to phone the airport and reserve a seat on the eleven o'clock flight to Boise. The timing would be close, but it was the only flight leaving that day.

The next problem was how to take along clothing for herself and Mike without arousing suspicion. The diaper bag could be filled with Mike's things, of course, since she would be expected to take it along even for a short trip to town. She finally decided to carry an overlarge shoulder bag, too, which would hold several more changes of clothing for Mike and a nightgown and toiletries for herself. She would have to borrow clothing from Jan for a few days.

Before going to the nursery she called Jan and told her she and Mike wanted to come for a visit. Jan welcomed them eagerly, vowing that she hadn't imagined how dreadfully she would miss Carrie and Mike until they had moved out.

With so many things to do, she had little time to think about how Josh would react to her disappearance until she was aboard the plane. She had directed Adam to drop her and Mike at the corner of the block where Julia Freemont's craft shop was located with the excuse that she needed something from the drugstore. When Adam had driven away, she walked around the corner to the town's only taxi company and took a cab to the airport.

Now, with Mike held securely on her lap and the plane lifting from the runway, she thought about Josh. She hadn't even left him a note. There hadn't been time; and, besides, what could she have written except what they both knew: their marriage had been a mistake. Carrie believed that Josh would probably be relieved to have her out of his life—but she had taken Mike. Once he had said to her: "If you ever decide to leave, Mike stays with me."

The fears that she had been too busy to acknowledge before came crowding into her thoughts. She had defied Josh, broken a promise to allow him to raise

Mike, and she knew him well enough to be certain that such betrayal would not be accepted without a fight. Clutching Mike to her, she tried to remain calm. She would have to fight Josh in court if it came to that. At least now, as Mrs. Joshua Revell, money was available to her, even if she had to depend upon the law to get it. But, dear heaven, she did not want to engage in a bitter wrangle with Josh in a courtroom.

She could not even bear to think about that and, opening a picture book she had stuffed into the diaper bag, she began to read a child's story to Mike.

They took a cab from the Boise airport to Jan's apartment, where Jan had left the door key beneath the hall mat as she had promised. Inside the apartment, Carrie walked through the small rooms, carrying Mike. It looked just as it had when she left it, and yet somehow everything was different. It wasn't that the apartment had changed, she realized, but she had.

She had left, against her will, on her wedding day, hating Josh and everything he stood for. She had returned with even more reluctance but because there seemed to be nothing else she could do. And during the past three months hate had turned into deep love, a love from which she knew she would never be free. She felt tears starting down her cheeks and went into the kitchen, where she wiped her eyes and found something for lunch.

Mike was still napping when Jan burst into the apartment after work. The redhead flung her fake fur coat aside and hugged Carrie tightly.

"Gosh, it's wonderful to see you! I'll bet Mike's asleep, but I can't wait to look at him." She tiptoed to the bedroom door and peeked inside. After a moment, she slid the door shut again and turned to Carrie. "How he has grown!"

"He's walking everywhere now," Carrie said. "I'm

glad you didn't get rid of his old crib. He went right to sleep, as if he were at home." She hesitated, realizing that this *was* Mike's home now, at least until she could find a place for them to live permanently.

Watching her, Jan frowned. "Well, tell me how long you can stay."

Carrie walked to the couch and sat down. She fingered the frayed piping on the arm. "Jan, I've left Josh. If you can put up with Mike and me until I can find a place, I'd be grateful."

Obviously stunned, Jan lowered herself slowly into a chair. "Left Josh? Do you mean for good?"

Carrie nodded. "I'm going to see a lawyer about a divorce as soon as I'm settled."

"But this is awful, honey. What happened?"

"I can't talk about it now, Jan. Maybe later."

"Sure," Jan agreed, curiosity and sympathy mixing in her expressive eyes. "I think I hear Mike. No, you sit. I'll go get him."

When Jan came back into the living room carrying Mike, the little boy looked about eagerly and said, "Daddy," in a mournful tone of voice. Jan glanced quickly at Carrie, who managed to divert Mike's attention with his picture book for the moment, knowing it was only a temporary diversion. He would ask for Josh again—and again. But he was so young that he would forget quickly, Carrie told herself.

The days in Jan's apartment fell into a pattern. While Jan was at work, Carrie cared for Mike as well as doing the laundry and preparing the meals for the three of them. After a couple of days, Carrie stopped expecting to see Josh every time someone came to the door or hear his voice whenever she answered the phone. She began to have misgivings, too, about leaving without telling anyone where she was going. Each day she told herself she must find a lawyer, but the days continued to come to an end without her having made any real effort to do so.

Sometimes she almost wished that Josh would call or come after them. Slowly it dawned on her that a part of her had half counted on Josh's love for Mike to bring him to Boise. She berated herself for such foolishness, telling herself that she *must* start divorce proceedings. But the next day she found another reason for not contacting a lawyer.

She and Mike had been living with Jan for more than a week when, early one afternoon while Mike napped, she heard a foot on the stair and knew immediately that it was Josh. She began to shake even before he rang the doorbell. Her first impulse was not to answer, to pretend no one was at home. But the impulse was fleeting and she knew that she must face him. He would not be satisfied until she did.

She opened the door. He stood in the shadowy hallway, and she realized in dismay that he looked ill. His face was paler than she remembered, the hollows in his cheeks were more pronounced, and the lines alongside his mouth were deeper than ever.

Carrie gazed at him with stricken eyes. "Josh . . ."

He walked past her without speaking, taking off his topcoat and dropping it on a chair, striding through the living room and glancing into the bedroom where Mike was sleeping. Then he turned back to Carrie, and there was something in his eyes that pierced her heart.

"How—how did you find us?"

"I have known all along that you were here. It was the only place you could have gone. Besides, I checked with the airline and was given your destination." This was said with little inflection as he shoved his hands into his trousers pockets.

"Why have you come?"

He did not answer immediately. Instead he walked

over to one of the windows overlooking the street and stared out, his back to Carrie. "I came to take you and Mike back home with me." He paused. "I just now realized how pompous that must sound. I can't force you to stay where you don't wish to be, can I?"

"I know that you love Mike," Carrie said quietly, her eyes resting on his slumped shoulders with heart-twisting love, "and I know that I promised I would never take him from you. But, Josh, I can't let him go."

He turned to look at her across the narrow expanse of the living room. "Yes, I love Mike and I want him back, but that can wait. Right now I want to talk about you and me, Carrie. Before you left there was so much that I wanted to say to you, but suddenly you were gone without a word to anybody."

She turned her glance away and moved to sit uneasily on the arm of a chair. "I'm sorry for that, Josh. I should have left a note or telephoned. I didn't know what to say. I decided it would be easier for both of us if I just left and got a divorce. I knew that's what you wanted, and—"

"Wait a minute." He frowned. "You thought I wanted a divorce?"

"Yes," she murmured, looking at her hands. "It was obvious that you were miserable."

"That, at least, is true," he said quietly.

She took a deep breath. "When I learned that you were spending more and more time with Jessica, I knew I was only in the way."

"Let me understand this," he said slowly. "Where did you get the idea I was spending so much time with Jessica?"

Carrie raised her head and met his scowling look. "Jessica told me. She came to the house to—to see your mother. She said you had been at her house only two nights before, and she left the impression that she saw you frequently—like that."

His scowl deepened. "I see. Well, I've been dense about Jessica. I did go by her house one evening that week because she called and asked me to come. She has been calling me frequently lately asking for my advice about various investments. That evening she wanted to know whether to sell some municipal bonds her husband had left her. I'm afraid it took me a long time to realize that her so-called interest in investments was really an excuse to see me. I don't know how I could have been so obtuse except that I've known Jessica for years and I just couldn't believe she would be so devious. It was only after you had left and she began to call even more frequently and drop by my office with dinner invitations that I saw where her real interests lay."

"But it's been so obvious ever since I married you that you and Jessica were—that you—"

"That we were lovers?" he said. "You accused me of that before, but I was never sure you really believed it." He paused and the silence hung heavily between them. "Carrie," he said finally, "I don't know what good it will do now, but I want you to know that my relationship with Jessica has always been friendship, nothing more. I don't love her. I never have. She may have led you to believe otherwise, but—"

"She did!" Carrie interrupted incredulously. "That afternoon when she came to the house she only came to tell me that you had been at her house. That's why I had to get out. I didn't know what to do. I—"

"That's why?" He stared at her. *"That's* why you left? Because of some lies that Jessica told."

Her breath quivered in her throat and she looked away from him, nodding dismally.

"Why couldn't you have come and asked me for the truth?"

Her chin came up and she met his look. "I don't know," she said. "Why did you stay at the office every night and let me believe you were with Jessica? You knew that I suspected you of having an affair with her. Why didn't you tell me otherwise?"

"Because every time we seemed to move a little closer to one another, you did something to make me angry. It always seemed to me that you did it deliberately," he said in low, bitter tones. "It appears that I have managed to do and say all the wrong things right from the start. That must be some kind of record."

She spread her fingers in a helpless gesture. "Josh, if only we could have talked about things. You must have known how insecure I was feeling. You made it clear that it was only Mike you wanted when we married. I even began to understand why he meant so much to you when Ethel told me that you lost your own baby, that Helen was carrying your child when she died."

"Helen wasn't carrying my baby."

"But your mother said she was pregnant," Carrie said, confused.

He stood looking at her for a moment, then he walked to the couch and sat down. He sat forward, his arms resting on his knees, and gazed at her. "Carrie, I think it is time we were honest with each other. I don't like to talk about Helen. I don't even like to think about her, but maybe I've been wrong in not telling you everything sooner. Helen was pregnant when she died, but it wasn't my child. She had been having an affair with a man named Darrell Wickersham for months before her death. He was a young doctor who was associated with Robert Marlow for a time. The child was Wickersham's. The two of them went to Toronto together. I'm sure they meant to stay there or somewhere in Canada. But they died in that fire."

Several things that had puzzled Carrie were beginning to come clear: the embarrassed silence at the table the night Jane Marlow mentioned Dr. Wickersham's name, Carrie's own feeling that it had seemed odd for

Helen to go to Toronto alone. . . . "Your mother must not have known that the baby wasn't yours."

Josh's lips twisted with irony. "I expect she is the only one in town who has never suspected the truth. She persists in believing that Helen had only gone on a short holiday and that, had she not died, she would have come back home."

"Josh, I know it's painful for you to tell me these things. You loved her very much, didn't you?"

His smile was faintly mocking. "I don't even know anymore. I suppose I did in the beginning, but I had stopped loving her long before she left me. Our last year together was hell. After she died, I vowed never to put myself at a woman's mercy again. Love wasn't for me."

"I see," she said in a small voice. "So you decided to marry me because I had Mike and you didn't even have to pretend to love me."

"Mike was part of it," he admitted, "but do you really want to know why I married you?"

She nodded reluctantly.

"I wanted to take you to bed."

She closed her eyes, her pulses hammering.

"When I walked in here that afternoon and saw you, I remembered that vulnerable young girl I'd met one evening at dinner with Danny and your sister and hadn't been able to get out of my mind for weeks afterward. When I saw you again, you were still young and vulnerable, but more beautiful than ever. I wanted you then, and I want you now. You are my wife, Carrie, and I can't let you go."

Carrie felt a shock run through her. She stared at him, her color fading. "What do you mean?"

Slowly he got to his feet and came across the room. He loomed over her, his tawny head bent. Then his hand came out and caught her arm, pulling her to her feet. "I've spent the past ten days trying to convince myself that I ought to give you a divorce if that is what you want. I know now I can't do it."

Carrie turned her head away, trembling. She felt confused, incredulous.

"Look at me, Carrie!"

Her lashes swept down over her eyes, resting against her hot cheeks, but she could not raise her head and let him see the unshed tears. His hand moved over her shoulder and along her neck, his thumb beginning almost absently to stroke her nape in a slow caress.

She was limp under his touch, and her eyes lifted slowly to his face questioningly. "What are you trying to say, Josh?"

The golden depths of his eyes had taken on a tormented look, and his mouth was compressed with intensity. "You know what I'm saying," he muttered.

"No," she whispered. "Tell me."

His fingers slid into the silky brown strands of her hair, caressing her skin. "You are determined to humble me, aren't you?"

She felt the blood racing through her veins as though some icy barrier had suddenly broken down. She was aware, with a thundering of her heart, of Josh's thickened breathing as he bent toward her, his mouth brushing her hair, her forehead, her cheeks.

She heard the hard intake of his breath, then he crushed her against him, his mouth seeking out hers relentlessly, a long-denied hunger surging out of bounds between them. She clung to him, winding her arms around his neck, her mouth responding eagerly under his, her fingers twisted in the thick tawny hair, pressing his head closer.

After a while he lifted his head and stared down into her face, his eyes devouring her. "I love you. I tried to tell you before, but could never say it."

She pressed her body against him. "Josh, darling . . ."

He buried his face against her throat, kissing it sensuously. "I love you," he murmured into her skin. "I told myself at first that I was marrying you for Mike's sake. You were the most physically desirable woman I'd ever known, but I convinced myself that's all it was. Do you remember when I took you home on our wedding day, when I kissed you in your bedroom? I knew then that I was starting to fall in love with you."

She blinked away tears of happiness. "Oh, Josh, I love you, too. That's why I couldn't bear staying with you, thinking that you were in love with another woman. Did you really love me on our wedding day? The first time you made love to me, you loved me then?"

He lifted his head and looked down at her adoringly. "That's when I knew I would always love you."

She hugged him fiercely, pressing her cheek against his shoulder. "Then it's all right," she sighed raggedly. "Our baby was made with love."

After a moment of sudden stillness, he turned her face up to his. "Our baby?"

She smiled. "I'm pregnant, Josh. It happened that first time." Then she sobered. "You don't mind, do you?"

"Mind!"

"It's so soon—"

His mouth cut off the words and she felt her blood catch fire under the possession of his lips. At last he whispered thickly, "We'll take Mike home, and then we'll spend a few days alone together at the family lodge in Sun Valley."

"Do you think it will be all right for me to ski in my condition?" she asked teasingly.

"You," he said thickly, "are going to have much better things to do than ski."

Carrie laughed and he lifted her into his arms. "Do you think Jan would mind if we borrowed her bedroom?" he whispered into her ear.

"I don't think she would mind at all," Carrie murmured and lifted her lips for the burning seal of his kiss.

Silhouette Romance

15-Day Free Trial Offer
6 Silhouette Romances

6 Silhouette Romances, free for 15 days! We'll send you 6 new Silhouette Romances to keep for 15 days, absolutely free! If you decide not to keep them, send them back to us. We'll pay the return postage. You pay nothing.

Free Home Delivery. But if you enjoy them as much as we think you will, keep them by paying us the retail price of just $1.50 each. We'll pay all shipping and handling charges. You'll then automatically become a member of the Silhouette Book Club, and will receive 6 more new Silhouette Romances every month and a bill for $9.00. That's the same price you'd pay in the store, but you get the convenience of home delivery.

Read every book we publish. The Silhouette Book Club is the way to make sure you'll be able to receive every new romance we publish.

This offer expires November 30, 1981

Silhouette Book Club, Dept. SBB17B
120 Brighton Road, Clifton, NJ 07012

Please send me 6 Silhouette Romances to keep for 15 days, absolutely free. I understand I am not obligated to join the Silhouette Book Club unless I decide to keep them.

NAME_____

ADDRESS_____

CITY_____STATE_____ZIP_____

Silhouette Romance

ROMANCE THE WAY
IT USED TO BE...
AND COULD BE AGAIN

Contemporary romances for today's women.

Each month, six very special love stories will be yours

from SILHOUETTE.

Look for them wherever books are sold

or order now from the coupon below.

$1.50 each

Silhouette Romance

#49 DANCER IN THE SHADOWS Wisdom	#66 PROMISES FROM THE PAST Vitek
#50 DUSKY ROSE Scott	#67 ISLAND CONQUEST Hastings
#51 BRIDE OF THE SUN Hunter	#68 THE MARRIAGE BARGAIN Scott
#52 MAN WITHOUT A HEART Hampson	#69 WEST OF THE MOON St. George
#53 CHANCE TOMORROW Browning	#70 MADE FOR EACH OTHER Afton Bonds
#54 LOUISIANA LADY Beckman	#71 A SECOND CHANCE ON LOVE Ripy
#55 WINTER'S HEART Ladame	#72 ANGRY LOVER Beckman
#56 RISING STAR Trent	#73 WREN OF PARADISE Browning
#57 TO TRUST TOMORROW John	#74 WINTER DREAMS Trent
#58 LONG WINTER'S NIGHT Stanford	#75 DIVIDE THE WIND Carroll
#59 KISSED BY MOONLIGHT Vernon	#76 BURNING MEMORIES Hardy
#60 GREEN PARADISE Hill	#77 SECRET MARRIAGE Cork
#61 WHISPER MY NAME Michaels	#78 DOUBLE OR NOTHING Oliver
#62 STAND-IN BRIDE Halston	#79 TO START AGAIN Halldorson
#63 SNOWFLAKES IN THE SUN Brent	#80 WONDER AND WILD DESIRE Stephens
#64 SHADOW OF APOLLO Hampson	#81 IRISH THOROUGHBRED Roberts
#65 A TOUCH OF MAGIC Hunter	

SILHOUETTE BOOKS, Department SB/1
1230 Avenue of the Americas
New York, NY 10020

Please send me the books I have checked above. I am enclosing
$_____ (please add 50¢ to cover postage and handling. NYS and
NYC residents please add appropriate sales tax). Send check or
money order—no cash or C.O.D.'s please. Allow six weeks for delivery

NAME_____

ADDRESS_____

CITY_____ STATE/ZIP_____